"Jake." The stern  planned to deliv
like an invitatio

One he accepted.

The instant their lips touched, Lilly surrendered to him. This was unquestionably a mistake and something she'd regret later. But for now, Jake's strong fingers kneading her skin through her shirt, his tongue and lips tantalizing her, were exactly the emotional balm she needed, and she took every ounce of comfort he was willing to give.

The blazing intensity of their kiss lasted several moments longer. Their mouths broke apart but not their embrace. He seemed to sense she needed more time before letting go. Sliding her hands to his shoulders, she waited for her breathing to calm.

At his next words, it stopped completely, and her limp hands fell away to land in her lap.

"Marry me, Lilly."

Dear Reader,

We often hear about books altering the course of people's lives. Perhaps it's even happened to you. It has me, and I can still remember the moment, though twenty-two years have passed since then. I was visiting a friend, and she lent me one of her many Harlequin books. I spent the next afternoon reading when I should have been working, never guessing at the profound effect this one book would have on me.

I'd always been an avid reader from the time I was young, but hadn't been drawn to romances. Obviously I didn't know what I was missing. From that day forward, romance books became my staple. I started out devouring…er, I mean, reading Harlequin Superromance novels. Then one day another friend gave me a Harlequin American Romance book she'd particularly enjoyed. It was to be another defining moment.

When I decided to pursue writing, I didn't pick romances—they picked me. Being published by Harlequin, who produced the books I enjoyed reading more than any others, became my dream— one I realized in 2006.

Harlequin books have changed tremendously since the time my friend lent me that first one, and I'm so excited and honored to be a tiny part of that revolution. Maybe one day a book of mine will land in someone's hands and alter their life. As a writer, I can't think of anything more rewarding.

Warmest wishes,

Cathy McDavid

Waiting for Baby
CATHY MCDAVID

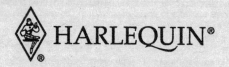

HARLEQUIN®

TORONTO • NEW YORK • LONDON
AMSTERDAM • PARIS • SYDNEY • HAMBURG
STOCKHOLM • ATHENS • TOKYO • MILAN • MADRID
PRAGUE • WARSAW • BUDAPEST • AUCKLAND

Recycling programs
for this product may
not exist in your area.

ISBN-13: 978-0-373-75268-3

WAITING FOR BABY

Copyright © 2009 by Cathy McDavid.

ABOUT THE AUTHOR

For the past eleven years Cathy McDavid has been juggling a family, a job and writing, and has been doing pretty well at it except for the cooking and housecleaning part. Mother of boy and girl teenage twins, she manages the near impossible by working every day with her husband of twenty years at their commercial construction company. They survive by not bringing work home and not bringing home to the office. A mutual love of all things Western also helps. Horses and ranch animals have been a part of Cathy's life since she moved to Arizona as a child and asked her mother for riding lessons. She can hardly remember a time when she couldn't walk outside and pet a soft, velvety nose (or beak, or snout) whenever the mood struck. You can visit her Web site at www.cathymcdavid.com.

Books by Cathy McDavid

HARLEQUIN AMERICAN ROMANCE
1168—HIS ONLY WIFE
1197—THE FAMILY PLAN
1221—COWBOY DAD

Don't miss any of our special offers. Write to us at the following address for information on our newest releases.

Harlequin Reader Service
U.S.: 3010 Walden Ave., P.O. Box 1325, Buffalo, NY 14269
Canadian: P.O. Box 609, Fort Erie, Ont. L2A 5X3

To Clay and Caitlin, my own precious babies,
who aren't so little anymore. I love you to pieces.

Chapter One

Lilly Russo wasn't looking forward to meeting with the man who'd so unceremoniously dumped her a mere three weeks ago. She'd do it, however, and just about anything else for the clients of Horizon Adult Day Care Center. They were too deserving, too much in need, too dear to her to lose out on a golden opportunity because of her pride.

"Mr. Tucker will be with you in a few minutes."

"Thank you."

If his assistant knew that her boss and Lilly had recently engaged in a brief affair, she gave no indication.

"Would you care for coffee or water while you wait?"

"I'm fine, thank you."

Lilly attempted a smile and sat on the closest piece of furniture, which happened to be an overstuffed couch, and instantly sank like a stone into its soft cushions. She should have chosen the chair by the window instead. Then she would've been able to stand gracefully when the assistant or, worse, Jake Tucker himself came to collect her for their appointment.

While she waited, she studied the comfortable and charmingly appointed lobby. The rustic, western flavor of the mountain guest resort was as apparent here as everywhere else on the ranch. Green checked curtains framed large picture windows. Heavy pine furniture, much of it antique, sat on polished hardwood floors covered by colorful area rugs. Paintings depicting nature scenes and wild animals indigenous to Arizona's southern rim country hung on the walls.

Lilly had been acquainted with Jake Tucker—manager of Bear Creek Ranch and landlord of the mini mall where the day-care center was located—for almost two years. They'd first met here in his office, when she'd become the day care's new administrator and her predecessor had introduced her to Jake. Since then she'd visited the ranch only a few times. But at the Labor Day cookout nine weeks ago, Jake had suddenly taken notice of her and asked her on a date.

If Lilly knew then what she did now, she'd have saved herself a heap of heartache and refused his invitation.

The assistant appeared in Lilly's line of vision. "Mr. Tucker will see you now."

She pushed out of the couch, wobbling only once, much to her relief. If it hadn't been so important to make a businesslike impression on Jake, she'd have worn something other than a slim-fitting suit and high-heeled pumps. He wouldn't guess by looking at her how much his abrupt breakup had hurt. Not if *she* could help it.

"Follow me, please." Jake's assistant led Lilly behind the busy front desk to an open office door. She gestured for Lilly to enter before discreetly moving aside.

The moment of truth had arrived.

Mentally rehearsing her pitch, Lilly stepped into Jake's office. She came to a halt when the door closed behind her. Lilly's stomach, already queasy to begin with, knotted into a tight ball.

Jake sat behind a large, ornate desk reading a computer screen, his profile to her. He turned his head to look at her, and she was struck anew by his intelligent hazel eyes and strong, square jaw. Memories of cradling that face between her hands while they made love flooded her.

She promptly lost track of what she'd planned to say.

He stood and extended his hand across the desk. "Good morning, Lilly. How are you?"

His greeting jump-started her befuddled brain. "Hello, Jake."

She stepped forward and accepted his handshake. His grip was confident and controlled and reminiscent of when their relationship had been strictly professional. But she'd seen him in those rare moments when he lost control and gave himself over to passion. That was the Jake she found most attractive, the one she'd fallen for harder than she would've thought possible.

"Thanks for seeing me on such short notice." She cleared the nervous tickle from her throat and sat in one of the two visitors chairs facing his desk.

"I would've come to the center on my next trip to town," he said, resuming his seat.

"I felt our meeting should take place here, since what I want to discuss involves Bear Creek Ranch."

"Is that so?" he asked and leaned forward.

He wore his sandy brown hair a little longer than when she'd first met him. It complemented his customary wardrobe of western shirts and dress jeans—and was surprisingly soft when sifted through inquisitive fingers.

"Yes." Lilly struggled to stay on track.

She couldn't afford to mess this up. The facility's clients and staff were depending on her to make their hopes and dreams a reality.

Besides, she and Jake weren't an item anymore, their personal relationship over. Hadn't he made that abundantly clear three weeks ago? He could get down on his knees and crawl across the floor and she wouldn't agree to see him again.

Lilly Russo didn't court misery. She'd already had enough in her life, thank you very much.

"As you know," she went on, finding her stride, "the center isn't just a babysitting service for emotionally and mentally challenged adults. One of our goals is to provide clients with recreational activities that enhance their life experience, either by intellectually stimulating them or teaching them skills they can use outside the center."

"You have a great program there."

"I'm glad you think so because we'd like your help with a project."

"What kind of help?"

Someone who didn't know Jake quite so well might have missed the subtle change in his expression from mild interest to wariness. Lilly suspected the wariness had more to do with his feelings toward her and their breakup than not wanting to help the center. She rallied against a quick, yet intense, flash of pain and continued with her pitch.

"The center's revenue comes from a variety of sources, including donations. Some of those donations are in the form of equipment or furniture or even small appliances rather than money. We've received an item that I initially thought was unusable. But after some consideration, I've changed my mind. Dave, our owner, and the staff, agree with me that if we can find a suitable place to board this…item, it might prove to be very valuable and enjoyable to our clients."

"Board?"

Trust Jake to pick up on the one key word in her long speech.

"Yes. A mule."

"Someone's given you a *mule?*"

"Tom and Ginger Malcovitch. You may know them."

"I do." Jake frowned.

Lilly knew why. Ginger's brother and Jake's ex-wife had

recently announced their engagement. In fact, it was right after their announcement that Jake had asked Lilly out on their first date.

Unfortunately, she hadn't seen the connection. Not until the night he'd ended their relationship.

She pushed the unhappy memories to the back of her mind, determined not to let anything distract her. "The mule is old and very gentle, though slightly lame in one leg. But not so lame that he couldn't be led around a ring carrying one adult."

"Your clients?"

She nodded. "I'm sure you've heard of the positive effect animals can have on the mentally, emotionally and even physically challenged. They seem to have an ability to bond with these individuals in a way people can't."

"I saw something on TV once."

"Yes, well, the benefits animals have on the elderly and disabled is a documented fact." She wished he'd sounded more enthusiastic.

"And you think this mule will help your clients?"

"I'm convinced of it." She gathered her courage. "In addition to corralling the mule with the horses on the ranch, we'd need to use your riding equipment. In exchange, our clients who are able to will do some work for the ranch."

"What kind of work?"

"Mucking out stalls. Feeding. Cleaning and oiling saddles and bridles. Whatever simple tasks can be accomplished in a morning or an afternoon."

"How often would you come out?"

"Three times a week. More if I can recruit additional volunteers."

Horizon employed ten full-time caretakers, including two nurses and several student volunteers from the nearby college.

Outings required one caretaker for every two clients and put a strain on the center's regular staff. She doubted Dave and his wife would agree to hire more employees.

Jake expelled a long breath and sat back in his chair.

Lilly sensed she was losing him and panicked. "I've spoken with our CPA. She tells me the cost of boarding the mule would be a tax deduction for the ranch."

"It's not just money."

"You've offered to help the center in the past."

"I was thinking more along the lines of repairs and maintenance. Not providing jobs for your clients."

"Work in exchange for boarding our mule isn't exactly a job."

"There's an issue of liability." Jake spoke slowly and appeared to choose his words carefully.

Lilly's defenses shot up. "Because they're disabled?"

"Because they'd be neither guests nor employees. I'm not sure they'd be covered by our insurance in the case of a mishap."

"Oh. Of course." Insurance wasn't an obstacle Lilly had considered, and she chided herself for her shortsightedness. "I understand. You have to do what's best for the ranch."

"I'll call our agent later today. Check with him on how the policy reads."

The wheels in Lilly's mind turned. "What if our insurance covered the clients while they were on the ranch?"

"Does it?"

"I'll find out. If not, maybe Dave could have a special rider added."

Jake drummed his fingers on the desktop. "Even if I end up agreeing to your proposition, I'll still need to take it to the family for their approval."

Here was an obstacle Lilly *had* considered. Jake managed Bear Creek Ranch but it was owned equally by eight members of the Tucker family, including him.

"I'd be happy to meet with them," she said, hope filling the void left by her earlier disappointment.

"Let's wait a bit. That may not be necessary."

She sat back in her chair, unaware that she'd inched forward.

"Your clients would also have to keep a reasonable distance from the guests. Please don't take this the wrong way, but they might make some people uncomfortable, and I have to put our guests' interests first."

Was Jake one of those "uncomfortable" people? Lilly compressed her lips and paused before replying. She encountered this discomfort on a regular basis. And not just at work.

It had started with her ex-husband, immediately following their son Evan's birth. She'd also seen it in the expressions of countless friends and relatives who had visited during the two months little Evan resided in the hospital's neonatal intensive care unit. Then later when they brought him home, still hooked to machines and monitors. The discomfort prevailed even at Evan's funeral seven months later.

Differences and abnormalities, Lilly had sadly learned, weren't always tolerated. All she could do was try to show people that special needs individuals were frequently affectionate and charming.

"That won't be a problem," she told Jake. "The people we choose to bring will be closely supervised at all times. At least one staff member for every two to three adults."

"That should be acceptable."

"Good." She made a mental note to contact the college regarding more student volunteers.

"I'll let you know what the family says." Jake rose.

Lilly did likewise. "Do you know when that might be?" She started to mention the Malcovitches impending house sale, then bit her tongue. Another reminder of Jake's ex-wife's engagement wouldn't advance her cause. "We need to find a place for the mule this week."

"Saturday's the earliest I can get everyone together. If you're stuck, you can board the mule here temporarily."

"Really?" She couldn't help smiling. His offer was both unexpected and generous. "Thank you, Jake."

He came around the desk toward her, a spark of interest lighting his eyes. "It was nice seeing you again, Lilly."

As they walked toward his office door, his fingers came to rest lightly on her elbow. The gesture was courteous. Not the least bit sexual. Yet, she was instantly struck with an image of that same hand roaming her body and bringing her intense pleasure.

Oh, no. She didn't need this now. Not when she'd finally resigned herself to their breakup.

"I'll call you in a day or two about our insurance policy." She casually sidestepped him, the movement dislodging his hand.

"Take care, Lilly."

Was that concern she heard in his voice? Did he regret the ruthless manner in which he'd informed her they were through? A more plausible explanation was that she'd only heard what she wanted to.

But then, there was that look on his face….

"You, too, Jake." She left his office before she could jump to a wrong conclusion, barely acknowledging the young woman seated at the workstation behind the front desk.

Lilly's thigh-hugging skirt hampered her hasty retreat across the lobby. She slowed before she tumbled down the porch steps. From now on, she vowed, whatever happened between her and Jake Tucker would be strictly business. Forget all those looks and touches and vocal inflections. She wasn't going to endanger a valuable program for the center. Nor was she risking her heart on the basis of a few misread signals.

* * *

BUTTONING HIS flannel-lined denim jacket, Jake headed out the main lodge and along the uneven stone walkway leading to the parking lot. A gust of wind swept past him, sending a small pile of leaves and pine needles dancing across the hard-packed dirt.

He held the crown of his cowboy hat, dropped his chin and walked directly into the chilly breeze. Fall came quickly to this part of the state and stayed only briefly before winter descended. Within the last few weeks, the temperature had dropped twenty degrees. By next month, frost would cover the ground each morning. Soon after that, snow.

Bear Creek Ranch was always booked solid during the holiday season, which stretched from late October through the first week of January. Nestled in a valley at the base of the Mazatzal Mountains, it was surrounded by dense ponderosa pines and sprawling oak trees. Bear Creek, from which the ranch derived its name, ran crystal clear and icy cold three hundred and sixty-five days a year. Fishermen, both professional and amateur, flocked from all over the southwest to test their skill at landing record-breaking trout.

Jake had lived on the ranch his whole life—until two years ago when he'd walked in on his then-wife with another man. Given the choice, he'd have sought counseling and attempted to repair his and Ellen's deteriorating marriage, for the sake of their three daughters if nothing else. Ellen, on the other hand, had wanted out and promptly divorced him.

Because he wanted his daughters to grow up in the same home he had, enjoy the same country lifestyle, remain near the close-knit Tucker family, Jake had let Ellen keep their house on the ranch until their youngest child graduated from high school. He'd purchased a vacant lot a few miles up the road. There, he'd built a lovely—and terribly empty—house on a hill with a stunning view no one appreciated.

Never once did Jake dream Ellen would bring another man into *his* home to sleep in *his* bed, eat at *his* table, live with *his* daughters. The very idea of it made him sick. And angry. That anger had prompted him to invite Lilly on a date.

Seeing her for the first time since he'd botched their breakup, watching the brave front she put on, had reminded him of the genuine liking he'd had for her and still did. He'd been a jerk for treating her so poorly—but not, he reasoned, for letting her go.

As difficult as their breakup had been for both of them, it was for the best. Jake had jumped the gun with Lilly, something he'd realized when she'd begun to pressure him for more of a commitment. His daughters were having trouble coping with their mother's upcoming marriage and the prospect of a stepfather. A new woman in Jake's life would've added to those troubles, and his daughters came first with him. He'd chosen wisely, he felt, to call it quits with Lilly before too many people were hurt or, as in her case, hurt worse.

Climbing into his pickup truck, he took the main road through the ranch to the riding stables. He pulled up beside a split-wood fence his grandfather had built fifty years ago and parked.

"Howdy, Jake." Gary Forrester, the ranch's manager of guest amenities, came out from the barn to greet him. He carried a metal toolbox in one hand. In the other, he jangled a set of keys to one of the ATVs the hands regularly used to get around the property.

"Hey, Gary. You off somewhere?"

"The number-three pump went on the fritz this morning. I'm on my way up the hill to see if I can talk sweetly to it." The older man had a real knack with finicky pieces of machinery, coaxing them to work when they were beyond repair. Hired thirty-plus years ago by Jake's grandfather, he'd become a permanent fixture on the place.

"I won't keep you long, I promise." Jake ambled toward the holding corral where a dozen horses milled quietly in the warm noontime sun. The other dozen or so were out carrying guests on one of the many scenic trails winding through the nearby mountains.

"I can spare a minute." Gary set the keys and toolbox on the ATV's wide seat and joined Jake at the corral. "What's on your mind?"

"Any chance we have room for another animal?"

"Sure. You found one?"

"Not exactly." Jake rested his forearms on the piped railing. "This one would be a boarder."

"Hmm." Gary raised his weathered brows. "That's a new one. Didn't think we were in the boarding business."

"We're not. The Horizon Adult Day Care Center has come by a mule and is looking for a place to keep it." Jake didn't need to elaborate. Gary was familiar with the center. It was located in the same small shopping plaza as the antique store co-owned by his wife and Jake's aunt. "An old, lame mule, so I'm told."

Gary pushed his cowboy hat back and scratched the top of his head. "What in the tarnation are they doing with a mule?"

"The Malcovitches donated it." The reminder of Ellen's fiancé triggered another surge of anger in Jake. He quickly suppressed it.

"Why?"

He summarized Lilly's plan to use the mule as a teaching tool and positive influence on the center's clients. "I haven't decided anything yet. There are some insurance issues to resolve. And I wanted to bounce the idea off you, seeing as the work the clients do will fall under your domain."

"Are them people up to the task? Cleaning out pens doesn't take much know-how, but it's physically demanding, and they gotta be able to follow directions."

"Ms. Russo seems to think they are." Jake's voice involuntarily warmed when he spoke Lilly's name.

Did Gary notice? Jake wasn't sure how much the employees knew about his former relationship with Lilly or what conclusions they'd jumped to. Bear Creek Ranch was a small community, and as much as the family tried to minimize it, people gossiped.

"What about the guests?" Gary asked.

"Obviously, nothing the center does here can interfere in the slightest with the ranch's operation."

Gary nodded. The guests—their comfort and enjoyment—were his top priority. "We might want to put the mule in by himself for a while. Just to be on the safe side. Some horses take unkindly to long ears."

"I don't think he should be allowed on any trails, either, until we determine just how lame he is. Make sure he's ridden only in the round pen for now."

"Sounds like you've already decided."

"No. But I will take Ms. Russo's proposal to the family."

Gary's eyes twinkled with amusement. "That ought to be interesting."

Jake didn't dispute his statement. The Tuckers were close but they didn't always agree on what was best for the ranch—and each other. Gary knew that better than anyone. Thirty years of working and living side by side with his employers had given him an inside track. Their relationship had recently become further entwined when Gary's daughter had married Jake's former brother-in-law.

"We're meeting on Saturday," Jake said. Pushing away from the railing, he turned toward his truck, mentally composing his argument to the family in favor of Lilly's plan. Tax deduction and goodwill aside, it was the right thing to do. The Tuckers had a longstanding history of giving back to the community.

"I'll have Little José ready one of the stalls," Gary said.

"No rush."

Jake's words were wasted on his manager. The stall would be fit for a Kentucky Derby winner by quitting time today.

"Not that my opinion counts, but I think helping the center is a good idea." Gary had fallen into step beside Jake. Midway between the ATV and Jake's truck, they paused to finish their conversation. "Ms. Russo is a fine lady with a heart of gold. She works her tail off for them folks."

"Yes, she does."

Was that a subtle reprimand in Gary's tone or was guilt coloring Jake's perception? Probably a little of both.

"Lord knows some of them need a fighter on their side. It'll be my pleasure having her around."

Jake's, too. More than he would've guessed and for reasons in no way connected to the center, its clients or an old, lame mule about to find a new home on the ranch if he had any say in the matter.

He cautioned himself to tread carefully. The reasons he'd broken off with Lilly in the first place hadn't changed. If anything, they'd intensified. As his ex-wife's wedding approached, his daughters were becoming more sullen and starting to act out, especially his oldest, Briana. Asking them to accept yet another change, in this case Lilly, wasn't fair and would only make the situation worse.

Lilly had the right idea: keep things on a professional level, for everyone's sake.

But after seeing her today, Jake knew it wouldn't be easy.

Chapter Two

Lilly bent over the compact porcelain sink and turned the right faucet on full blast. Forming a cup with her hands, she splashed cold water on her face. A quick glance in the mirror confirmed that her efforts fell short of the desired effect. Her complexion remained as pale as when she'd woken up that morning.

With a flick of her wrist, she shut off the water, snatched a coarse paper towel from the dispenser and blotted her face dry. When she was done, she reached into her purse and removed a small bottle of antacid tablets, popping two in her mouth. She doubted they'd cure what ailed her.

Since last Thursday when she'd met with Jake, her stomach had been in a chronic state of queasiness. Despite her best efforts, her plan for the center still hadn't come together. And at the rate things were progressing, it might never.

Keeping her word to Jake, she'd contacted the Horizon day care's owners over the weekend, and Dave had assured her the insurance was adequate to cover clients and staff while they were visiting the ranch. Yesterday afternoon, the appropriate documentation was faxed to Jake's office. His assistant had verified its receipt but volunteered no additional information in response to Lilly's probing, other than to inform her that Jake would be in touch.

Lilly's anxiety had increased when the Malcovitches called a short while ago to tell her that if she didn't have the mule picked up by tomorrow, they were giving him to someone else. She immediately placed another phone call to Jake and received the same cryptic message from his assistant. Lilly's nerves couldn't take much more.

Popping a third antacid tablet, she returned the bottle to her purse and silently chided herself for letting Jake's failure to call back upset her to the point of making her ill. He'd said he'd be in touch and he would. Jake was nothing if not dependable. All she had to do was wait.

Giving her wispy bangs a quick finger-combing, she spun on her heels, opened the bathroom door and was immediately halted in midstep. Mrs. O'Conner was right outside and standing behind her wheelchair was Georgina, the center's head caregiver.

"Sorry." Georgina backed up Mrs. O'Connor's wheelchair to let Lilly pass. "She says she has to go. Now." Georgina rolled her eyes.

Lilly understood. Mrs. O'Connor "had to go" five or six times a day, whether she truly needed to or not.

"How are you doing today, my dear?" Lilly stooped to Mrs. O'Connor's level and laid a hand on her frail arm. "You seem sad."

Mrs. O'Connor raised watery eyes to Lilly. "My cat's missing."

"Oh, I'm sorry to hear that."

"She's been gone three days now." Mrs. O'Connor sniffed sorrowfully. "Such a good kitty."

Lilly straightened but not before giving the older woman a reassuring squeeze. "I'm sure she'll return soon."

"I hope so."

According to Mrs. O'Connor's daughter, the cat had ex-

pired of old age more than a year earlier. There were days Mrs.
O'Connor remembered and days she didn't. The Horizon
staff had been asked by her daughter to play along whenever
the cat was mentioned.

The O'Connors were typical of the center's clients. Caring
for elderly and emotionally or physically challenged adults
wasn't always easy. Families needed breaks to run errands,
attend to personal business, go to dinner or one of a thousand
other things most people took for granted. If family members
worked outside the home, those breaks were even more important. The Horizon Adult Day Care Center helped by providing
quality care in an attractive facility and at an affordable price.

After the death of her son, Evan, and the divorce that
followed, Lilly had reevaluated her priorities and decided on
a change in careers. The satisfaction she derived from earning
a fat paycheck and driving a nice car waned in comparison to
making a difference in people's lives. At first, she'd contemplated working with children but that would have been too difficult. When she heard about the administrative position at the
Horizon Center, she knew she'd found what she was looking
for. Accepting the position, she left her job at Mayo Clinic
Arizona and moved from Phoenix to the considerably smaller
town of Payson.

There'd been times during her thirty-two years when Lilly
was happier, but never had she felt more valued or appreciated.

"Do you need any help?" she asked Georgina.

"I think we can manage." Maneuvering Mrs. O'Connor's
wheelchair to clear the bathroom doorway, Georgina set about
her task with the cheery smile that made her such an asset to
the center.

"If my daughter phones about my cat, will you come get
me?" Mrs. O'Connor called as the door was closed.

"Right away."

Lilly traveled the short hall that opened into the main recreational room. There was, as usual, a flurry of activity and a cacophony of noisy chatter. She was stopped frequently—by both clients and staff members—on the way to her office, located near the main entrance.

"Lilly, Mrs. Vega has taken the TV remote again and refuses to tell me where she's hidden it."

"Try looking in the microwave."

"M-M-Miss R-R-Rus-s-so. S-s-see wh-what I d-d-draw."

"Very nice, Samuel."

"The soda machine is out of Pepsi again."

"You know you're not supposed to drink caffeine, Mr. Lindenford. It makes you agitated."

And on it went.

Lilly's official title was administrator, which involved running the office, supervising the personnel, maintaining the financial records and overseeing customer relations. Some days, however, she felt more like a babysitter. Not that she minded.

Lilly no sooner reached the entrance to her office door and sighed with relief when she was stopped yet again.

"Is it true we're picking up the mule tomorrow?"

She spun around. "Jimmy Bob, where did you hear that?"

The young man hung his head in shame. "Georgina told me."

He was lying. They both knew it. Like many people with Down's syndrome, Jimmy Bob was a sweet, kind soul with boundless energy and a quick, hearty laugh. He was also a chronic eavesdropper, sneaking quietly up and listening to conversations that weren't any of his business. Because it was impossible for him to keep a secret, he always confessed what he'd heard, usually in the form of a lie so as not to implicate himself. Fortunately, he was also very likeable.

Lilly took pity on him. His woe-is-me expression never failed to win her over despite resolutions to the contrary.

"Sucker," she mumbled under her breath, then said out loud, "We *hope* to be able to pick up the mule tomorrow. We're not sure yet."

"When will we be sure?"

A glance at the phone on her desk and the glaring absence of a flashing red message light made her heart sink. Jake still hadn't called. Was he avoiding her? Had the family rejected her plan, and he was trying to think of an easy way to let her down?

"I don't know, Jimmy Bob. By the end of today, maybe, if all goes well."

His face broke into an enormous grin, his earlier shame evidently forgotten. "Can I ride him tomorrow? I'm a good rider. Ask my mom. She took me riding at the ranch. You know, the one with the big white barn." He started whistling an off key rendition of the theme to *Bonanza.*

Bear Creek Ranch had a red barn. Jimmy Bob must be referring to Wintergreen Riding Stables, which were located about a mile outside town heading toward Phoenix.

"*If* we get the mule and *if* your mother agrees, you can ride him. But that won't be tomorrow, honey."

Jimmy Bob stopped whistling and his enormous smile collapsed.

"Maybe by Friday." She patted a cheek that bore severe acne scars along with the slightest hint of facial hair. "I promise, when we finally take our first trip to see the mule, you'll go with us."

She meant what she'd said. If Jake agreed, they would need their more able-bodied clients to keep Horizon's end of the bargain. Jimmy Bob wasn't only enthusiastic, he was strong and fit and cooperative. Other clients, like Samuel, weren't capable of performing any chores but would be able to interact with the mule, possibly ride it while being led around a ring.

Jimmy Bob's smile showed signs of reemerging.

"Would you do me a favor?" Lilly asked.

He bobbed his head.

"Go to the supply closet and bring me a ream of paper, okay?"

He shot off to do her bidding. Lilly didn't really need a ream of paper. She had two stacked beside her printer from previous attempts to distract Jimmy Bob.

Sitting at her desk, she debated placing another call to Jake and was startled when the phone rang. It was answered by Gayle who was currently manning the welcome desk in the main room. The four to five caregivers always on duty took turns at the desk, rotating every hour or so. Ten seconds later when the caller wasn't put through to her, Lilly gave up hope that it was Jake.

She lifted a manila folder from a wire rack on the corner of her desk and withdrew the monthly bank statements. Normally, she could reconcile a bank statement in her sleep, but today the numbers refused to add up. Her chronic indigestion wasn't helping matters. How long until those damn antacids kicked in?

How long until Jake called?

Lilly jumped to her feet. It wasn't quite lunchtime, but she couldn't tolerate the waiting anymore. A break from the center might be the perfect remedy to settle her nerves. She stopped at the welcome desk to inform Gayle that she was leaving.

But Gayle forestalled her. "Any chance you can postpone lunch a few minutes?"

"Why?" Lilly inquired.

She inclined her head in the direction of the front door. Lilly turned to see Jake striding across the room straight toward her.

JAKE SENSED every pair of eyes on him but he didn't react.

Activity and chatter ceased by degrees until the hiss of a

wheelchair-bound woman's portable oxygen tank was the only sound in the room. Three people abruptly leapt out of their seats to trail his every move, like predators stalking prey. He looked behind him and smiled. One of the trio, a young man, smiled back. The other two glared openly. Jake was an experienced businessman and accustomed to holding his own under pressure. But for some reason, his confidence wavered, and he didn't like it.

"Good morning, Lilly," he said when he reached her.

"Hi, Jake."

"Are you all right?"

"I'm fine."

She didn't appear fine. Fatigue shadowed her eyes and when she first caught sight of him, her cheeks had paled. Shock at seeing him? He supposed he should have called first. But the family trust attorney's office was only a few minutes away, and since a signature was required on the contract, Jake had decided to stop in and deliver it in person.

His self-appointed security detail crowded in around them. Jake shifted, resisting the urge to tug on his suddenly tight shirt collar. If Lilly noticed, she gave no indication.

"Is there somewhere we can talk?" Glancing around, he added, "Alone."

"Come with me." She motioned for him to follow. His security detail came, too. Once he and Lilly had crossed the threshold into her office, she informed the group to "Wait here" and shut the door on their unhappy faces. "Sorry," she told Jake. "New visitors always create a stir. They weren't intentionally ganging up on you."

"No problem." When she didn't stop scrutinizing him, he added, "Really."

"Don't be embarrassed. Special-needs individuals often make people feel ill at ease."

"I'm not ill at ease."

She didn't believe him. He could tell by her narrowed eyes.

Could it be true? Jake didn't consider himself a snob but the fact was, he'd had little interaction with "special-needs" people other than his grandfather. Jake had been away at college during most of Grandpa Walter's decline and, as a result, missed the worst of it.

"I'm—" he started to say ignorant then changed it to "—inexperienced."

"You're not alone." She didn't act offended at his remark. Quite the contrary. "Would you like a tour of the facility?" Pride rang in her voice. "You're our landlord, after all, and I don't think you've seen the place since I took over."

What she said was true. With the exception of his aunt's antique store located in the same plaza, Jake rarely dropped by his tenants' businesses. Not unless there was a problem, which wasn't the case here. And during the short time he and Lilly had dated he had always picked her up at her house rather than work. He'd told himself it was a matter of convenience for both of them, as most of their outings took place in town. Now he wondered if he hadn't been unconsciously keeping their relationship from progressing by avoiding her work and the ranch.

"Thanks, but I can't." He hated disappointing Lilly. She obviously loved the center and showing it off. "I'm meeting someone for lunch, and I only have a few minutes." As if a switch had been flicked, she sobered, and Jake didn't know why. Had he insulted her by declining her offer of a tour? He certainly hadn't meant to.

"Please, sit." Lilly gestured at the visitor's chair facing her desk.

"I'd rather stand if you don't mind. I've been sitting all morning and will be again all afternoon."

Her office had a glass window opening out to the main

room. He turned to face it, and a dozen heads swivelled to stare at him. The young man who'd smiled earlier waved exuberantly. Without thinking, Jake raised his hand in return.

"Did you get the insurance certificate we faxed over?" Lilly asked.

"Yes. It's exactly what we needed." He stepped away from the window and held out the envelope he'd been carrying. "Our attorney also suggested we draw up a contract."

"Does that mean…" She took the envelope and turned it over in her hands. "Has the family agreed?"

"For once, we were completely unanimous." Jake hadn't needed to twist one arm or press a single point. "I didn't tell you earlier because I couldn't meet with our attorney until this morning."

"Oh, wow." Lilly's face, always so expressive, lit up. "I can't believe it."

Her delight was contagious, and he chuckled. "There are one or two conditions you should know about."

"Oh?"

Jake sobered. He hadn't yet determined how he felt about the stipulations the attorney had insisted on putting in the contract. "As you can imagine, liability is our main concern. Our attorney suggested that someone in charge, specifically you or the owner, accompany the clients on their visits. At least for the first several months until we determine how well the program is going."

"I doubt Dave can go. He and his wife commute regularly to Apache Junction where they just opened a second center."

"Then I guess it'll have to be you."

He could see the uncertainty in her eyes and wondered if she harbored the same doubts he did about the prospect of them constantly running into each other at the ranch.

"Okay." She nodded resignedly. "Whatever it takes."

"You sure?"

"Positive." She relaxed. "I'm not about to let a few scheduling conflicts get in the way of this program."

"I'm glad."

"Thank you, Jake." Setting the envelope on her desk, she took a step toward him, and hesitated. Then, evidently going with her first instincts, she closed the distance between them. "Thank you so much."

Before he could say anything, she linked her arms around his shoulders. He automatically returned the hug and was instantly lost when she laid her head in the crook of his neck. They had, after all, done this before. Often.

He might have gone on holding her, might have let himself enjoy the memories her nearness evoked, if not for a loud bang on the window. Lilly gasped and sprang back. Jake swung around to see what had caused the noise.

One—no, make that two dozen—of the center's clients and staff stood crowded outside the window, some with their noses or fingertips against the glass.

"Are we getting the mule?" The young man's muffled shout barely penetrated the insulated window.

Lilly nodded, fidgeting nervously. Her previously pale cheeks shone a vivid red.

Their audience cheered. Lilly motioned for them to go on about their business. Her order went unheeded. "Now," she mouthed, and still no one moved.

Jake couldn't help himself and laughed.

"This isn't funny," Lilly scolded and retreated behind her desk.

He could see her point, though for a moment or two, it had been nice holding her.

"What next?" she asked him and glowered at the window. Some of their audience had fortunately dispersed. The rest ignored her silent warning and remained glued to the spot.

"You and Dave review the contract. If it meets with your approval, sign it and send it to my office."

"What about the mule?"

"I'll arrange to have him picked up, unless you have access to a truck and horse trailer."

"We don't."

"Is tomorrow early enough? I remember you said you were in a hurry."

"Tomorrow's perfect. I'll let the Malcovitches know."

The reference to his ex-wife's fiancé's family didn't generate nearly the anger it usually did. If anything, Jake felt good. Damn good. His charitable deed accounted for some of his elevated mood. He suspected Lilly's hug was responsible for the rest.

"I have to leave. I'm late for my meeting."

"I'll walk you out." She came around from behind the shelter of her desk.

At the entrance to the center, he got another hug. This one, however, was from the young man who'd waved. Not Lilly.

JAKE WATCHED Lilly's long legs emerge from the open car door. Her delicate shoes were sexy as hell and completely inappropriate for traipsing around a stable. Her wool slacks weren't much better. At least she'd had the sense to wear a warm coat. She must have flown out the door and sped the entire drive from Payson, considering what good time she'd made.

"Is that him?" she asked. Breathless and eager, she tentatively approached the mule tied to the hitching post in front of the barn. Her long black hair, usually twisted in a braid or gathered in a ponytail, fell loose around her shoulders, framing her face and emphasizing her large brown eyes.

"It is." Jake couldn't look away. Only after he'd stared his fill did he invite her to come and stand by him. Together, they turned their attention to the ranch's newest boarder and the man standing beside him. "That's Doc Mosby. He's giving the mule a quick examination."

"He's not sick?"

"Just a precaution." Jake stooped to pick up an empty feed bucket and set it on one of the grain barrels. "Our attorney suggested the mule be vet-checked on arrival and regularly after that, since he's lame."

"Oh." Lilly observed the vet at work, her brow knitted with worry. "Did you receive the contract?"

"Our attorney's still reviewing the changes your boss made."

"Oh," she said regretfully. "I was hoping to get started by Friday."

"Even if the contract's not finalized, you can bring a small group on Friday morning to see the mule and tour the stables."

"Not to sound ungrateful because I truly appreciate this, but how big is *small?*"

"No more than six clients at a time."

"Another of your attorney's suggestions?"

"Don't be mad. It's his job to watch out for the family and the ranch."

"I'm not mad. If six is our limit, then that's what we'll bring."

The vet was bent over, one of the mule's hooves braced between his legs. Using a pick, he dug around inside the hoof. Jake and Gary had their own suspicions about what had caused the animal's lameness. It would be interesting to see if the vet also concluded it was a deformity.

"Doc Mosby was out here anyway to examine one of our pregnant mares," Jake explained to Lilly. "I'll just have him add the charge for Big Ben to his bill. Your clients can work it off, along with the other expenses."

"Big Ben?"

"That's the mule's name."

A smile touched the corners of Lilly's mouth. "It fits."

Jake agreed. The mule stood as tall as any of his horses and was considerably wider than most. "My guess is his mother was a draft horse."

"What kind?"

"A Belgian. They're similar to the Budweiser Clydesdales you see in the TV commercials, only sorrel."

"And sorrel is?"

"The color of his coat. A kind of red like Big Ben. Clydesdales are usually a darker shade of brown."

She sighed miserably and shook her head. "I think I might've gotten myself in over my head. Everything I know about horses and mules could fit into a thimble."

"You'll do fine." He smiled encouragingly. "And we have plenty of experienced ranch hands around to help."

"I hope it wasn't too much of an inconvenience to pick up Big Ben today," she said, changing the subject to a safer one.

"Not at all. I sent Little José."

"Make sure you add that expense to the others." She gave a small laugh. "At this rate, we'll be here every day for a year working off our bill."

Against his better judgment, Jake was liking their arrangement more and more. He seized the chance to study her while her attention was on Doc Mosby and the mule.

At the time of their breakup, Jake had been completely positive that continuing their relationship was a mistake. He liked Lilly and hadn't wanted to string her along when there was no hope whatsoever for a future together.

That hadn't been his initial feeling, though. In the beginning, their dating arrangement had been exactly the enjoyable distraction he'd needed to take his mind off his ex-wife's engagement and help him move on. But things had quickly become complicated, in large part because of his daughters, although they weren't the only obstacle.

Once he and Lilly became intimate, the complications increased. Not because there was anything wrong with the sex. Quite the opposite, in fact. But Lilly didn't give herself to just anyone. Sex came with a commitment from her *and* him.

Jake had held her in his arms after they made love that last time, stared into those gorgeous brown eyes that brimmed with hope and expectation and realized, with a sinking heart, that he couldn't offer her what she wanted, what she needed. Not anytime soon. To continue as they were would have been unfair to Lilly. So, instead of postponing the inevitable, he had broken up with her the following day, telling himself he'd done it for her sake.

But after their meeting in his office last week, it had occurred to him that his actions weren't entirely noble and were calculated to spare *him* grief, not her.

"Good boy." Doc Mosby dropped Big Ben's hoof and patted his round rump, then came over to chat with Jake and Lilly.

"Lilly, this is our vet, Dr. Greg Mosby," Jake said. "Lilly Russo is the administrator of the adult day care center that owns the mule."

"Nice to meet you." Doc Mosby pulled a handkerchief from his back pocket and wiped his hands before shaking Lilly's.

"What do you think?" Jake asked.

"Well, I'd say he's in pretty good shape overall. A little fat—" Doc Mosby patted his protruding stomach "—but aren't we all? I suspect he's been standing in a pen too long. Exercise should shave off a few of those extra pounds."

"How lame is he?"

"Some. Corrective shoeing will help. He was born with a slight deformity to his right front hoof, and it's gotten worse with age. It causes his foot to turn in." Doc Mosby demonstrated with his hand.

"A birth defect?" Lilly's interest was visibly piqued, which, in turn, piqued Jake's.

Doc Mosby grinned. "I reckon you could call it that."

"If you want to return him to the Malcovitches—"

"No, no!" Lilly cut Jake short. "He's perfect for us. A mule with a birth defect helping people who are themselves physically challenged."

"Have your farrier insert a leather wedge between the shoe and the hoof," Doc Mosby explained. "It should straighten the hoof and reduce the pain."

"Can he be ridden before then?"

"I wouldn't recommend it."

Lilly's smile dimmed.

Jake touched her arm. "I'll call the farrier, have him come out here Friday morning. That way, the people in your program can watch Big Ben being shoed firsthand."

She instantly brightened. "Oh, that would be wonderful!"

Clapping the vet on the shoulder, Jake gestured at Gary with his other hand. "You ready to look at that mare?"

"Sure."

Gary, who'd been standing nearby, took charge of the vet, leaving Jake alone with Lilly.

"Is it all right for me to pet Big Ben?" she asked.

"Would you like to walk him to his stall?"

"Yes!"

Jake went over and untied the mule's lead rope. Big Ben ambled obediently alongside Jake, his large feet clip-clopping in the dirt.

"Here."

She took the rope. Bunching it in her fingers, she gazed up at Jake. "What now?"

"You walk, he follows."

"Just like that?"

"With him. Not so with all horses or mules. But this guy's a teddy bear."

"I walk." She took a tentative step.

"That's it."

"He's not following."

"Keep going."

She did. The heels of her completely inappropriate shoes wobbled and dust coated her expensive slacks. Big Ben finally extended one foot and lifted his huge head to snuffle her hair.

"Hey! That tickles." Lilly raised her hand, not to push the animal away but to stroke his nose.

Big Ben snorted and nuzzled her cheek, clearly enamored.

He wasn't the only one.

Jake found himself attracted to Lilly all over again.

He would have to watch himself closely in the coming weeks and months. Lilly deserved more than he could give her. She deserved a man ready, willing and able to commit.

Chapter Three

"Put your seat belt back on, Jimmy Bob."

"But we're here."

Lilly turned around and gave the young man a hard stare. She sat in the front passenger seat of the center's specially modified van. Beside her, driving the van, was Georgina. The student volunteer accompanying them sat in the rear.

"Not yet," Lilly told Jimmy Bob. "We just pulled in to the ranch entrance. The stable is another mile from here."

Jimmy Bob rarely rebelled but he did so today, his normally cherubic face set in stone, his arms folded. Lilly attributed his stubbornness to excitement. Since he'd learned yesterday morning that he'd be one of the six people accompanying Lilly on the center's first trip to see Big Ben, he'd been bouncing off the walls. His high-strung behavior earned him frequent reprimands from the staff members and his family. This morning, he'd reached emotional overload, becoming surly and rebellious. Not uncommon behavior for individuals with Down's syndrome.

Lilly couldn't allow Jimmy Bob to ignore the rules, today or any other day. Anyone riding in the van obeyed them or wasn't permitted to go on the next outing.

"Pull over," she said.

Georgina slowed and eased the vehicle safely to the side of the bumpy dirt road. She knew the drill, and once they were stopped, she put the van in Park and shut off the ignition.

"Damn it to hell, Jimmy Bob," the woman sitting beside him shrieked. "Put your freakin' seat belt on."

"Don't swear, Miranda," Lilly scolded.

"He's screwin' it up for everybody." Jimmy Bob's seatmate clutched the sides of her head in an exaggerated display of theatrics. A lock of wildly curly hair had come loose from her ponytail and stuck up like a rooster's comb.

"Jimmy Bob," Lilly implored in a tone that was midway between firm and coaxing.

"Can I ride the mule first?"

"We're not riding Big Ben today. The farrier has to put new shoes on him."

"When we do get to ride the mule, can I be first?"

"Oh, puleeze!" Miranda banged her head repeatedly against the padded rest behind her. "Quit being such a damn baby."

"Miranda. You're not helping." Lilly aimed a warning finger at her.

Miranda slapped a hand over her mouth to muffle her groan.

Lilly cautioned herself to remain calm. Though her patience was often tested by the people in her care, she hardly ever lost it. Had her son lived, she would've made a good mother.

Her throat closed abruptly and tears stung her eyes. Lilly didn't know why. It had taken a while, but in the two and a half years since Evan's death, she'd finally stopped crying at every reminder of him.

"What's wrong, Miss Russo?" Jimmy Bob didn't miss a thing.

"Nothing."

He grabbed his seat belt and buckled it. "I'm sorry. I didn't mean to make you mad at me."

"I'm not mad." She smiled at him, still fighting her unexpected weepiness. What had come over her today and why?

She wondered if seeing Jake so often lately and the memories stirred by those encounters had anything to do with her fragile mood. Lilly had come to care deeply for him during the six weeks they'd dated, which was why she'd pressured him for a greater commitment, ultimately triggering their breakup. And as much as she'd wished things could be different, she was afraid her feelings for him were as strong as ever.

Visiting the ranch two or three times a week wasn't going to be easy and made her wish that her boss was around more to share the responsibility.

Georgina started the van and pulled back onto the road.

"It's about freakin' time," Miranda exclaimed, flinging her arms every which way.

Lilly didn't react to the outburst, which was done solely to attract attention. She spent the rest of the drive preoccupied with her own thoughts. Maybe Jake wouldn't be there. He'd informed her that his manager, Gary Forrester, would oversee their visits and the chores they performed.

She'd just about convinced herself that the likelihood of running into Jake was nil when the stables came into sight— and so did his familiar pickup truck.

Lilly's heart involuntarily raced. With anticipation, not dread.

Georgina parked next to Jake's truck. Jimmy Bob was first out the door. No surprise there. Lilly went around to the side of the van and, along with Georgina and the student volunteer, helped the remaining five clients out.

"Stay together."

She'd gone over the rules with each of them repeatedly. Nonetheless, she anticipated disobedience. Jimmy Bob didn't disappoint her.

"Look! There's the mule."

"Jimmy Bob, come back!

Big Ben was tied to the same hitching post as the previous day. Tail swishing, he stood calmly, demonstrating what Lilly hoped was a personality ideally suited to her clients. He didn't so much as blink when Jimmy Bob came charging at him.

"Hey! Don't ever run up to an animal like that. You'll get yourself kicked."

The reprimand came from a teenage, female version of Jake. His oldest daughter, Briana. Lilly recognized her from the Labor Day cookout at the ranch. The girl cut in front of Jimmy Bob before he reached the mule. The young man came to a grinding, almost comical, halt.

"Just because an animal looks calm," Briana scolded Jimmy Bob with an authority beyond her years, "doesn't mean he is. Be careful."

He gazed down at her, slack-jawed.

"Did you hear me?"

"You're pretty."

She shook her head and huffed in exasperation. "Come on," she said after a moment. "I'll introduce you to Big Ben."

Jimmy Bob followed like a devoted puppy.

Lilly considered intervening, then decided against it. Jake's daughter seemed capable of handling herself, and while Jimmy Bob might be stubborn sometimes, he was trustworthy and didn't have a mean bone in his body.

"Are you ready, Mr. Deitrich?" Lilly shoved the sliding van door closed after the elderly man had climbed out.

"Where are we?" He gazed around in obvious confusion.

"Bear Creek Ranch. Remember? We're here to visit our mule, Big Ben."

"There are no mules at Gold Canyon," he scoffed. "Everyone knows the old man won't have the sorry beasts. Claims they scare the cows."

"We're not at Gold Canyon Ranch." She grasped his arm securely and guided him toward the mule, where the rest of their group had gathered to gape in awe. At a respectable distance, thanks to Briana. "We're at Bear Creek Ranch."

Mr. Deitrich had Alzheimer's disease. It began when he was in his early sixties and, sadly, progressed rapidly. During his youth, he'd worked on a cattle ranch in Wyoming. His wife hoped the familiar setting of stables and horses would stimulate him mentally and possibly improve his condition.

Lilly didn't know if it would work, but was more than willing to try. As the only adult day care center of its kind in town and with a wide variety of client needs, Dave and the staff were open to any new ideas and approaches. It was one of the reasons Lilly had fought so hard for Big Ben.

"Does anyone know the difference between a horse, a donkey and a mule?" Briana stood with a hand on Big Ben's neck, conducting class. "No? Well, a mule has a donkey father and a horse mother."

"She's always liked being in the spotlight."

Lilly whirled around to find Jake standing behind her and sputtered a startled, "Hi."

"I hope you don't mind Briana helping. She's off school today for some reason."

"Not at all." Lilly tried to focus on the teenager and not her father, who, like Lilly, stood to the side.

Briana was so much like Jake, in looks and mannerisms and personality. She even pursed her lips in concentration the same way he did before answering the many questions her audience threw at her. Clearly she was knowledgeable about horses and happy to share that knowledge with others. Jake must have been very proud of his oldest. Lilly certainly would be if Briana were her daughter.

Suddenly a lump formed in the back of Lilly's throat and

tears pricked her eyes. She blinked to counter the effect. What in the world was wrong with her today? Feeling vulnerable and not understanding why, Lilly hugged herself hard—only to let go with a small gasp that Jake fortunately didn't hear.

Her breasts hurt. A lot.

How strange was that? She'd noticed a tenderness this morning when she'd put on her bra but forgot about it in the next instant. Casting a sideways glance at Jake, she hugged herself again. Her breasts were definitely sore.

She must be having a raging case of PMS, she decided. That would explain her weepiness and the mild off-and-on stomach upset she'd been experiencing. Or maybe her birth control prescription needed adjusting. She hadn't responded well initially to the pill she was on and required several dosage modifications. What other explanation could there be?

Unless she was pregnant...

"Here comes the farrier," Jake said, nodding at an old pickup truck rumbling down the road.

Lilly composed herself and muttered, "Great." Swallowing did nothing to relieve the dryness in her mouth.

She couldn't be pregnant. It simply wasn't possible. She was on the pill *and* Jake had used condoms. Well, except for that one time when they'd gotten carried away in the hot tub at his house. But it shouldn't matter; the pill was nearly one-hundred-percent effective if taken every day, which she did without exception.

There had to be another explanation. Besides, she'd had her period a couple of weeks ago. Granted, it was a few days late and lighter than normal, but still a period. She'd even endured her usual cramping the day or two before.

"Who's ready for a tour of the stables?" Briana's question was met with great enthusiasm from everyone, especially Jimmy Bob, who was glued to her side. "Okay then, stay together. No wandering off. And no talking to the guests."

Lilly knew she should go with the group but her feet refused to obey her brain's command. When Jake tapped her on the shoulder, she practically jumped out of her skin.

"I'm going to talk to the farrier. Be back in a few minutes."

"Sure." She smiled weakly.

Watching Jake stride off, she decided that if she didn't feel better by tomorrow, she'd call her doctor and make an appointment. Another change in dosage, another switch to a different brand of pill and she'd be back to her old self.

She continued to delude herself for the rest of the morning and several days after that until it became impossible.

"How COULD THIS have happened?"

"The pill isn't infallible. And you only began taking it shortly before becoming intimate."

"He used a condom." *Most of the time.*

"They break. Leak. Come off."

"You've seen my records, you know my history. Before Evan, I had two stillbirths. One at five and a half months, the other at seven." Lilly's voice rose in pitch with each sentence she uttered.

Her doctor's voice, on the other hand, remained calm. "One thing you have to remember, Lilly, is this baby has a different father. The trisomy disorder that affected your previous children may have been a fluke combination of your DNA with your ex-husband's."

Lilly lifted her head, which had been propped in her hand, to meet Dr. Thea Paul's intense yet compassionate gaze. She liked the ob/gyn, who was a plain old small-town doctor and not a specialist in some obscure field of medicine Lilly didn't understand. She'd certainly had her fill of those back in Phoenix.

"I'm the carrier." She sniffed and wiped her damp cheeks. The emotions she'd been attempting to hold at bay overwhelmed her, and she blubbered, "That's what the other doctors told us."

Her fault the babies died. *Her* corrupt DNA.

It was why she'd vowed never to get pregnant again, why she was so diligent about birth control—at least, she'd *meant* to be diligent.

Dr. Paul got up from her chair, came around her desk and sat in the chair adjacent to Lilly's. She took Lilly's hand in hers. "Science and medicine aren't exact. I'm sure the other doctors explained your odds of having a healthy baby."

"Fifty-fifty. But that's not how it turned out." The chromosomal abnormality Lilly had passed on to her babies occurred only in males.

"Nature isn't exact, either," Dr. Paul said.

"I had my period." Lilly still resisted.

"Spotting, even heavy spotting, in the first trimester is common and can be confused with menstrual flow."

She wasn't reassured. Spotting and cramps had plagued her other three pregnancies. Accepting the tissue Dr. Paul offered, she blew her nose.

"This is all so…unexpected and…upsetting." She sobbed quietly. "God, you must think I'm a terrible person. All your other patients are probably thrilled to learn they're pregnant."

"Of course I don't think you're terrible," Dr. Paul said soothingly. "You've been through a lot and have every reason to worry about the health of your baby. There are several tests you can have that will determine—"

"No tests. They're too risky."

"Some are, that's true, but they can help you make an informed decision."

Lilly had heard of two patients at the hospital where she'd worked who'd miscarried after having amniocentesis. "There's only one decision to make. I'm having the baby."

Lilly's personal beliefs wouldn't allow her to terminate her pregnancy. It had been a contentious issue between her and Brad and a contributing factor to their divorce. When she became pregnant a second time, he'd insisted she undergo every available test.

She did as he'd asked. The results had revealed that the baby, also a boy, suffered from the same genetic disorder as his brother. After much pressure, Lilly succumbed to her husband's wishes and went so far as to schedule the termination but changed her mind at the last minute, to her husband's fury. For two long, agonizing months she carried the baby, knowing his chances of survival were slim to none but praying for a miracle.

The stillbirth broke her heart and nearly shattered her spirit.

With Evan, she'd stood her ground and refused all testing. What was the point when an abortion was out of the question? Fear and anxiety were her constant companion during that third pregnancy but so was hope for a girl and a different outcome. She wouldn't trade that feeling for the world, then *and* now.

"Your decision, of course." Dr. Paul squeezed Lilly's fingers. "And you can always change your mind later on."

"I won't."

Dr. Paul reached for Lilly's paperwork and made some notations. "You feel strongly now, which is understandable. That may change, however, when you talk to the baby's father."

Jake!

Lilly had been so busy the last few days denying the possibility of pregnancy, she hadn't considered what to tell him. Admitting her condition would be bad enough, especially when she'd assured him she'd been using birth control. Admitting the fact that their baby could be born deformed—if she even carried to term—was unimaginable. And grossly unfair to Jake. She knew firsthand the difficulties and potential agony facing them. He didn't. Worse, she was taking away his choice in the matter by choosing to have the baby regardless of his feelings.

"I can't tell him." She swallowed another sob. "Not yet."

"I'm your physician," Dr. Paul said. "It's not my place to advise you on personal matters. But as the father, he does have a right to know about the baby."

For one wild second, Lilly contemplated hiding her pregnancy from Jake. Then she remembered her agreement to accompany the center's clients on their visits to Bear Creek Ranch. He was no stranger to pregnant women and no dummy. He'd eventually figure out her condition and realize he was the father.

"I need some time before I make any announcements." There was so much to consider. Her job. Her family. The expenses not covered by her health insurance. Astronomical medical bills had also contributed greatly to her marital problems with her ex-husband.

And then there was Jake.

Lilly started to rise. Her unsteady legs refused to support her, and she immediately dropped back into the chair.

"That's a good idea. And do think about the tests. I would be remiss in my duties if I didn't advise you to have them." Dr. Paul handed Lilly several sheets of paper. "Take these to the front desk. The nurse will call in your prescription for prenatal vitamins."

"Thank you." Lilly tried again to stand and managed it this time.

"Since you're a high-risk pregnancy, I'd like to see you every two weeks if your schedule allows it."

Lilly nodded and stumbled out of Dr. Paul's office. She paid her bill, scheduled her next appointment and gave the nurse the name and phone number of her pharmacy, all in a daze.

The ground blurred on her walk across the parking lot to her car. She was barely aware of the return drive to the center and was surprised to find herself parked in her reserved space.

Sitting behind the steering wheel, she waited before leaving the car. Carefully, as if the slightest touch might harm the life growing inside her, she rested a hand on her abdomen.

Another baby. The last thing in the world she wanted, and, at the same time, the one thing she wanted with a longing that bordered on desperation.

A tiny seed of hope took root inside her. Was Dr. Paul right? Would this baby be born normal because the father was someone different? The tiny seed anchored itself more securely and began to blossom, filling Lilly with something she hadn't felt since her first pregnancy.

Joy.

A smile curved the corners of her mouth. The sigh escaping her lips was one of contentment, not despair. With a sense of elation, she opened the door and stepped out of the car.

She'd done no more than place one foot on the asphalt when the first cramp hit. The second was so severe, Lilly doubled over. Her breath came in spurts.

"Oh, God," she cried to herself. "Not again." Then, in a whisper, she pleaded, "Please don't take this baby from me, too."

Chapter Four

Jake looked up just as the beam from a pair of headlights cut across his kitchen window. Ellen was dropping off the girls for their regular Wednesday-night dinner—late as usual. He didn't have to worry that she'd come inside. His ex-wife avoided him if at all possible these days, for which he was grateful.

He'd no sooner taken dinner from the oven than the girls tumbled through the back door. In the next instant, their lively antics filled the room, and Jake's loneliness vanished.

"Cheese pizza!" LeAnne shouted and ran immediately to the table, where Jake had set out paper plates and napkins.

"What? No hug?"

His youngest fled the chair she'd been ready to occupy and bounded into his arms. At seven, she was mostly arms and legs and long auburn hair that refused to stay out of her face. Briana and his middle daughter, Kayla, quickly followed suit.

Jake cherished his girls and had bent over backward to preserve his relationship with them during his divorce from their mother. At the time, it had rankled to give in to Ellen's outrageous demands, especially since she'd cheated on *him*, not the other way around. Now he was relieved that Ellen was unable to engage him in her petty power plays.

"Who else besides LeAnne is hungry?" Jake reluctantly released his children.

"Me." Kayla scrambled to beat her sisters to the table.

Jake cut the pizza into slices and served it. He wasn't much of a cook, usually taking his meals with either employees or guests in the spacious dining hall. After the divorce, he'd learned to prepare simple meals for himself and his daughters. Kayla and Briana were both picky eaters—Kayla hated vegetables and Briana didn't eat meat—which made the task a daunting one at times.

"How's school?" he asked once they were all seated.

His question earned him a round of frowns and one dismal head shake.

"You always ask the same thing," LeAnne objected.

"I'm interested." Jake washed his pizza down with a glass of fruit punch, something the younger girls loved and he tolerated.

"Mom's taking me into Payson tomorrow after school to get my learner's permit."

At Briana's announcement, Jake choked. He'd known this day was coming but it still took him by surprise. "Driving? You're only fifteen!"

"Fifteen and seven months. Which is when I can legally get my permit."

"Can I ride with Briana?" Kayla piped up.

"Absolutely not." Jake massaged a throbbing temple. When had his baby girl become old enough to drive? "Maybe I should go with you."

"It's all right. You don't have to."

Briana was being too blasé, a sure sign of something amiss. "I want to go," he said, applying pressure with the skill of an experienced parent. "It's a big day for you."

"What about work?" Panic widened her eyes.

Eyes, he suddenly noticed, made to look larger by mascara, their lids faintly tinted with blue shadow. He didn't recall giving Briana permission to wear makeup. Obviously, her mother hadn't seen the need to consult him on the matter.

"I'll leave early," he answered, searching for other unwanted signs of maturity, like piercings and tattoos and hickeys on her neck. Fortunately, there were none, or else she wouldn't be getting her learner's permit for another ten years.

"Really, Dad. It's okay."

He recognized that tone. Whenever he heard it, a sour taste filled the back of his mouth. "Travis is going," he said flatly. "Isn't he?"

All three girls stopped eating in midbite. Briana stared at her plate, guilt written all over her face.

Jake set his paper napkin on the table although he would've preferred to pound his fist against the unyielding surface. His ex-wife's fiancé was accompanying his daughter to get her learner's permit. The son of a bitch. Where did he get off? He wasn't Briana's father. He wasn't even her stepfather. Not yet.

"Please, Daddy." Briana's voice fell to a whisper.

Translation: *Don't ruin this for me.*

"No. I'm sorry, honey." Jake could stomach a fair amount of insult but he drew the line at this.

"You promised I could get my permit as soon as I was old enough. And I've been studying for the test."

Though he recollected no such promise, he didn't dispute his daughter. Obtaining her learner's permit wasn't the issue. Rather, it was who went with her to the Department of Motor Vehicles. Or, more correctly, who *didn't* go with her.

"Fine, you can get it tomorrow."

"I can?"

"As long as Travis doesn't go with you. Your mother can take you. Alone," he stressed. "Or I will."

"Then you can take me." Briana's anxiety fled in an instant. She didn't care who went with her, only that she got to go.

"I'll call your mother and tell her."

Jake knew it wasn't fair of him to put Briana on the spot like this, yet he'd do it again in a heartbeat. Travis might be sleeping in Jake's bed but he sure as hell wasn't about to usurp Jake's place at his daughter's side during those all-important milestones.

"And I'd really prefer that only your mother or I give you driving lessons. Our insurance doesn't cover Travis."

"Yes, sir," Briana answered, cheerful once more. "I really didn't want him to go anyway."

In another moment, all three girls were eating and chatting as if no tense words had been spoken.

"What are you doing Friday after school?"

"I'm going to Mindy's for a sleepover," LeAnne said after a sip of fruit punch that left a pink mustache above her upper lip.

"I have an orthodontist appointment." Kayla peeled back her lips to show off her recently acquired braces.

Jake had foolishly hoped his daughters would be free and that he could squeeze in an extra visit this week. So much for spontaneity.

"What about you, Briana? We could have a driving lesson around the ranch. Early, before it gets dark."

"I...um..." She snapped her mouth shut, her indecision plain as day.

"Never mind," Jake grumbled. If she was going somewhere else with her mother and Travis, he didn't want to hear about it.

"She's giving riding instructions to those funny people with the mule," LeAnne piped up.

"Don't call them funny," Briana retorted hotly.

"Your sister's right, sweetie. That's not very nice."

LeAnne glanced around the table in a bid for support. "Well, they are."

Jake didn't know what baffled him more. Briana sacrificing her precious social time to work with Lilly's clients, or her quick and emotional defense of them.

"That's very good of you. I'm sure they appreciate it." Of his three daughters, his oldest was the only one to take a real interest in horses and the ranch.

"She spends practically every day there," LeAnne said with the conspiratorial demeanor of someone revealing a secret.

"Really?"

Jake hadn't been to the stables to check on Lilly's group in over a week. Not since last Tuesday when she'd acted so odd. He'd shown up, determined to be friendly and courteous, but drawing the line there. She'd appeared equally determined to avoid him and did everything from making flimsy excuses to turning on her heel and changing direction when she saw him coming. He eventually got the hint and made his own excuse to return to the office.

He hadn't spoken to her since, although he knew from Gary's reports that she'd accompanied her clients the required number of times as stipulated in their agreement.

What had brought about the sudden change in her? Had she sensed his lingering interest and decided to put a halt to it before things heated up again? If that was true, she had good reason to avoid him. He'd hurt her badly and too recently for her to have fully recovered.

Unless it was the other way around.

Could her abrupt retreat be because *she* had a renewed interest in *him* and didn't want to risk more heartache? While that scenario was somewhat tempting, he knew better than to consider it even for a moment.

"So I like giving riding instructions," Briana said, her tone defensive. "What's wrong with that?"

LeAnne shuddered. "They're strange."

"They have special needs." Jake stood and began clearing the table. He tapped Kayla on the shoulder and pointed to the refrigerator. She rushed over, opened the freezer compartment and gave a delighted squeal when she discovered the carton of ice cream he'd bought for dessert.

"I don't care," LeAnne continued with the typical unrestrained candor of a child. "They make me feel weird. Don't they make you feel weird?" She waited for Jake to answer.

He was torn between being honest and being diplomatic. Admittedly, there had been one or two moments at Horizon when he'd experienced some discomfort and one or two instances at the ranch last week when he'd had to force himself not to stare. It took an exceptional person to work with special-needs individuals, someone with an enormous capacity for caring.

Like Lilly.

"You feel a little weird at first," Briana said, showing a capacity to care as enormous as Lilly's. "But then you get over it and realize they're okay."

"She's right," Jake immediately agreed. "And what she's doing is very commendable." His gaze traveled from LeAnne to Kayla. "Don't either of you give her a hard time."

They nodded in synchronized solemnity.

"How 'bout you come with me on Friday?" Briana asked cheerfully. "You haven't been to the stables in a while."

"Sure." Jake smiled and dished out the ice cream. "I'd love to."

If he took Briana up on her offer, he'd get to spend extra time with her. Be a proud and doting father. Show his younger daughters that, like their sister, he accepted special-needs individuals. Also important, he'd see Lilly and reaffirm with her—and himself—that their relationship was strictly business.

His smile grew. Between going with Briana tomorrow to get her learner's permit and to the stables on Friday, the rest of the week was shaping up quite nicely.

"L-LOOK AT ME, Miss R-Russo. I'm r-riding."

"You're doing great, Samuel."

Lilly waved at the beaming man who clung to the saddle horn for dear life. His undersized body rocked back and forth in rhythm to Big Ben's slow steps. They'd had quite a time getting Samuel to wear a helmet; he didn't like anything constricting on his head. He'd finally relented when someone else nearly got his turn on Big Ben.

Jimmy Bob led the mule and rider around a circular pen, his smile equalling Samuel's in size. There wasn't anything about the ranch Jimmy Bob didn't love. Even the dirtiest, most backbreaking chores were completed with enthusiasm.

"Keep up the good work," Lilly hollered to both men, pleased with Samuel's progress and his growing confidence.

So far, everything about the center's new program met or exceeded the staff's expectations. The clients were responding well to the mule and he to them. Corrective shoeing had helped with his limp, enough so Big Ben could be ridden for two hours at a stretch without tiring. Not that they worked him hard. Mostly he walked. Slowly. Twice, Jimmy Bob got the mule to trot a few paces and yee-hawed like a wild cowboy when he did. Big Ben responded with his usual calm.

It had required some trial and error, but they'd developed a successful routine, thanks in part to Jake's daughter, Briana, who'd generously spent several afternoons with them. She or one of the hands helped them groom and saddle Big Ben. Then each of the six clients was given a twenty-minute ride on the mule, always under the supervision of two people, one from the center and one from the ranch. Anyone not riding was assigned chores, also under the same supervision guidelines. When they were done, Big Ben was brushed down and returned to his stall, where he was duly rewarded with carrots and petting.

After a week and a half, the group from Horizon had figured out the chores, which mostly involved cleaning stalls and pens and raking the barn aisle. Lilly appreciated Jake's kindness. She didn't think they were anywhere close to earning back Big Ben's board or the wages he paid the ranch hands who helped them.

At the thought of Jake, she automatically glanced over her shoulder to search for any sign of his pickup truck. He hadn't dropped by to watch them since the Tuesday after her doctor's appointment, when she'd received the startling news that she was pregnant.

A baby. Lilly still couldn't believe it.

There'd been no more cramps since that last incident in her car, and she'd had no spotting like in her previous pregnancies, and every morning when she woke up free of pain, she thanked God with all her heart.

As the baby's father, he has a right to know.

Dr. Paul's words resounded in Lilly's head. Despite that, she'd decided to wait until her fourth month to tell Jake. What would be the point if she lost the baby in the early stages?

You're scared, she told herself.

Yes, she was—scared of telling Jake and, even more, of losing the child who'd already become so precious to her.

"Have you seen Briana?" Jimmy Bob asked when he and Samuel passed the railing where Lilly stood.

"I don't know if she's coming today."

"She said on Wednesday she'd be here after school."

"It's still early. Maybe she's not home yet."

Lilly had only the briefest glimpse of Jimmy Bob's crestfallen face before he and Samuel passed out of range. She worried a little about Jimmy Bob's adoration of Briana, concerned the teenager might unwittingly hurt the young man if he got carried away—as he often did. Jimmy Bob's affection knew no bounds. Lilly made a mental note to keep tabs on the budding friendship, prepared to step in if necessary.

Hearing the rumble of an approaching vehicle, she turned and suffered a moment's confusion at seeing Briana behind the wheel of Jake's truck. Hadn't he come with his daughter? And since when did she drive?

Then, when the truck pulled in to an empty spot, she saw Jake in the front passenger seat, motioning with his hands and giving Briana what appeared to be parking tips. After a moment, they emerged from the truck and headed toward the barn.

All at once, Jake looked Lilly's way.

Instantly, every nerve in her body went on high alert. Her eyes shot down to her waistline. Not that she was showing yet. At seven weeks, her clothes had barely started feeling tight. Still, she was glad her bulky coat completely concealed her upper half.

Loosening her fingers from their death grip on the pipe railing, she reminded herself to stay calm. No reason to assume Jake was here to see her, especially after her cool treatment of him the previous week.

She hadn't meant to be ill-mannered but having only learned about the baby so recently, she'd been in no frame of mind to deal with Jake and the ever-present attraction she felt when they were together.

Her hopes of escaping his attention—if that was indeed what she wanted—were dashed when he changed direction and walked straight toward her.

"They look like they're having fun." He nodded at Jimmy Bob and Samuel, who were making yet another round of the circular pen.

"They are. Very much."

He didn't wait for an invitation, simply stood beside her as if she'd been waiting for him all along. So close, his arm inadvertently brushed hers when he moved. The touch was no more than a whisper but enough to make Lilly keenly aware of his proximity.

Had she ever reacted like this with her ex-husband? Probably. At least in the beginning, when their relationship was new and thrilling. Sadly, they'd forgotten that initial magic in the wake of endless heartbreak and disappointment. Not to mention financial pressure. Had even one small thing gone differently, they might still be married.

But then Lilly wouldn't be pregnant now and hoping against all hope that a different gene combination would swing the odds for a healthy baby in her favor.

Then what? Either way, healthy baby or not, Jake would have a role in her life—a significant one.

"Can any of your clients drive?" Jake asked.

Lilly brushed a lock of wind-blown hair from her eyes, using that as an excuse to mentally regroup before answering. "Some of the older ones may have had a driver's license years ago but I doubt they're allowed on the road. If they were, they'd be capable of independent living and wouldn't need our services."

"I was talking about a tractor here, around the ranch."

"Hmm. I don't know."

"Does he drive?" Jake indicated to Jimmy Bob.

"He hasn't mentioned it, and trust me, Jimmy Bob would." Lilly's involvement in the lives of their clients was restricted to Horizon and what was in their files or told to her by them in the course of a normal work day.

They watched Briana show Samuel how to hold on to the reins properly and sit straight so his shoulders weren't hunched.

Though standing and not riding, Jimmy Bob mimicked his friend.

"Do you think he'd like to learn?"

"I'm sure he would. The question is, would his parents consent?" She angled her head slightly to stare fully at Jake, something she'd been avoiding since he'd arrived. "What exactly are you getting at?"

He shifted and either consciously or unconsciously narrowed the space between them. Her awareness of him immediately intensified.

"We're short one hand this week. Little José went home to El Paso for his great-grandparents' fiftieth wedding anniversary. We need someone to drive the tractor and pull the flatbed trailer behind it."

"I…um…" Lilly wavered. Jimmy Bob's Down's syndrome wasn't as severe as most, but his capabilities were still limited.

"A tractor's much easier to operate than a car, and there's no traffic to contend with."

"Someone would have to teach him. Someone with a lot of patience."

"I had Briana in mind." He grinned. "She just got her learner's permit yesterday. I think she'd enjoy being the one giving instructions rather than taking them for a change."

"Is she competent enough? You said she just got her permit."

"That's true but she's been driving ATVs and the tractor around the ranch for years."

Lilly considered her concerns about Jimmy Bob's fondness for Briana. "A staff member would need to supervise them."

"Absolutely."

"And what about our agreement? Driving ranch equipment isn't in it. I'll have to check with our insurance agent about our coverage."

"I'll do the same. And amend our agreement if necessary."

"It's really up to Jimmy Bob's parents."

"Can you call them tomorrow? We're in a bit of a bind and could use his help. The Weather Channel's predicting rain, and we have to move the hay into the barn," Jake added by way of explanation.

"I guess I could."

Lilly was a little baffled by Jake's request. According to the terms of their agreement, the center's clients were obliged to perform whatever reasonable chores he or his manager asked of them. Filling in for an absent hand didn't strike her as particularly unusual. But she couldn't shake the notion that he had something else in mind.

"Seriously, do you really need Jimmy Bob? Don't you have plenty of ranch hands to drive the tractor?"

"Sure, but I thought he might enjoy it. And I want to set a good example for LeAnne and Kayla. They're both a little…shy about special-needs individuals."

Lilly was touched. "That's very nice of you, Jake."

"If you're not too busy afterward," he said, his tone casual, "I have some ideas I'd like to run by you."

"About our agreement?"

"Yes. And a few other things, too."

"Okay." She remained dubious, not sure how she felt about being alone with Jake.

"We can use Gary's office."

"I need to—"

Her sentence was cut short by a stabbing pain in her lower abdomen.

No! Not here, not now. *Not again!*

A second pain followed the first one. She didn't need to see her face to know all color had drained from it. While not terrible, the cramps were unexpected and alarming and too much like the ones preceding her previous stillbirths. She fought the wave of mild dizziness overcoming her. Only her hand on the railing kept her from swaying. Tears filled her eyes, distorting her vision, and she uttered a small cry.

"Lilly, are you all right?" Jake's arm circled her waist.

"I, ah…" A third cramp robbed her of further speech. Vaguely she realized people were staring.

So, apparently, did Jake.

"Come on. Let's get you out of here."

Jake guided her toward the barn. Lilly didn't object. Without thinking, she leaned into him and rested her cheek on his jacket sleeve. Instantly, she relaxed. A minute later— or was it several minutes?—a door appeared in front of her.

She glanced around, recognizing the room as an office. By the time he lowered her to a threadbare flowered couch, her pain had diminished, along with the dizziness.

Thankfully this episode, like the one in the parking lot the other day, hadn't lasted long or been too severe.

"You can stop fussing over me," she mumbled. "I'm fine."

"No, you're not." Stretching out her legs, Jake grabbed an old blanket, folded it into a square and positioned it under her raised feet. "You're pale, perspiring and shaking like a leaf."

"Am I?" Lilly touched her forehead and found it damp. "It's a little warm in here."

"Yeah, must be all of fifty-six degrees."

"Really, I'm okay." To prove it, she propped herself up on one elbow. "I had a charley horse in my leg, that's all."

He sat on the edge of one couch cushion and studied her intently. "Are you sure?"

She nodded, unable to verbalize another lie while he was staring at her with that concerned look in her eyes.

"Hey, boss. Is Ms. Russo all right?" Gary Forrester, Jake's manager, stuck his head in the door. "Want me to call 9-1-1?"

"No," Lilly insisted before Jake could answer.

"Give us a minute," Jake told Gary. "And pull my truck around if you don't mind."

"What for?" Lilly asked.

"In case I need to drive you to the emergency room."

"That won't be necessary." What she really wanted was to phone Dr. Paul and get her opinion before being rushed— again—to the emergency room, only to be sent home after several hours with instructions to rest and see her doctor the following day.

She refused, however, to call Dr. Paul in front of Jake.

"Just do it." He nodded at Gary who promptly left, closing the door behind him.

It suddenly occurred to Lilly how small the office was and how close she and Jake were on the couch. Not counting her impulsive hug at the center, they hadn't been this intimate since their dating days.

"I'd like to try sitting up," she said and struggled to get her balance. Jake helped by holding on to her elbow. His strong grasp felt familiar and reassuring. "Thank you," she said once both her feet were settled on the wood floor.

"Can you walk to the truck?"

"I'll be fine in the van."

"You're not going back to the center."

"Truly, I'm okay." She pushed off the couch. "See?"

She stood a total of two seconds before another cramp hit. She cried out, more in surprise than agony, just as Jake caught her and eased her onto the couch again.

"That's it. I'm taking you to the hospital now." He held her protectively, both arms around her.

"I want to call my doctor first."

"Your doctor? Damn it, Lilly, what's wrong?"

The combination of pain and fear and hormones and Jake

was too much, and she started to cry. Before she knew it, the words spilled from her mouth. "I'm pregnant."

Jake stiffened, although he didn't withdraw.

Lilly wiped her eyes with the back of her hand. For better or worse, he knew about the baby. As the cramp waned and her breathing returned to normal, she waited for his reaction.

Chapter Five

"How far along are you?"

"About nine weeks."

Jake stared at the winding mountain road and tried to recall a time he and Lilly had failed to use protection. There'd been that one night in the hot tub at his place. He hadn't worried much because she'd sworn up and down the first time they made love that she was on the pill.

"Nine weeks," he repeated and calculated dates. Definitely the night in the hot tub.

Not two weeks later, he'd ended their relationship. Had she known then she was pregnant? Probably not. Something told him she was every bit as shaken by this turn of events as he was.

"When were you planning on telling me?"

He'd insisted on driving her home—would have driven her to Payson and the emergency room if her cramps hadn't subsided. A phone call to her doctor had eased their anxiety. Dr. Paul had prescribed complete bed rest for twenty-four hours and told her to go to the E.R. only if the camps continued or if Lilly began to spot. She further assured them by saying she'd call Lilly at home to check on her later that evening.

Lilly had initially refused Jake's offer of a ride home, citing the center's policy that two staff members had to accompany clients on field trips at all times. He countered by suggesting Briana go with Georgina in the van. Lilly finally relented, but only after additional persuasion by Jake and Georgina.

He and Lilly had spent the first half of the twenty-minute drive in complete silence. Jake had needed the quiet to recover from his initial shock. Even now he wasn't entirely ready to talk, but he knew they should.

"To be honest," Lilly said, her face toward the passenger window, "I was going to wait until I reached my fourth month, when I started showing. Around the middle of January."

"January!"

"The chance of a miscarriage lessens after the first trimester. If I…if anything happened—"

"You had no right to keep this from me." He hadn't meant to snap and instantly regretted his tone. "I'm sorry. I'm still trying to cope with…the news."

The baby. Why couldn't he say the words?

Because he'd just learned that he was going to be a father again.

"I don't blame you for being angry." She abandoned the passing scenery to look at him. "I didn't deceive you intentionally. I really was on the pill and I'm as shocked as you are."

"I'm not angry. Just upset. You should've told me from the start."

"I practically did. I've only known about it for the past two weeks."

"Come on. You said it yourself. If not for your cramps, we wouldn't be having this conversation until January."

She didn't disagree.

"Are you planning on keeping the baby?" he asked after a moment.

"Yes."

"I'll help." He wasn't sure what he could do; they had a lot of decisions to make. But he'd be there for Lilly and their child, before and after the birth. "If you need money—"

"At this point, money isn't the issue. It's whether or not I can carry to term." Her eyes suddenly misted with tears. "Or how long the baby will survive after the birth."

"Why wouldn't the baby survive?"

"The other three didn't."

Jake's hands froze on the wheel. He quickly corrected his steering when the passenger-side tires went off the road and onto gravel. "You've been pregnant before?"

She sniffed and dabbed at her eyes with the back of her hand. "The first two babies were stillborn, one at five and a half months and the other at seven. A blessing in disguise. At least that's what well-meaning people told me. My son, Evan, lived. His deformities weren't quite as severe as his siblings. But the machines could only do so much, and he didn't reach his first birthday."

"Good God, Lilly. I'm so sorry." She'd told him about her former marriage. Not a single mention, however, of stillbirths or a son. "Can I ask what was wrong with him?"

"All three of my children had a trisomy disorder. Most of their major organs didn't work right or, in some cases, were missing. Their limbs were also shrunken and their heads mis-shapen from tumors." Her voice became flat and robotic, as if she was trying to distance herself from what she was saying. "The cause was a chromosomal abnormality. Faulty DNA. Mine, to be specific. My chances of having a healthy baby are supposedly fifty-fifty. So far the odds haven't been in my favor."

"That must've been really hard on you." He winced at his lame and grossly inadequate response.

Lilly didn't seem to notice. Or maybe she'd already heard the same thing a thousand times before.

"I didn't plan to ever get pregnant again," she said sadly. "I went so far as to schedule the procedure to have my tubes tied, but chickened out at the last minute."

"Maybe this time you'll get lucky."

She turned back to the window. "It's easy for people who have healthy children to say that."

"You're right. I was thoughtless. The fact is, I can't begin to imagine what you've had to endure or how I'd act in your shoes."

She didn't respond, and they drove the remaining three miles to Lilly's house in silence. Jake wasn't finished talking but didn't pressure her to continue. He figured they both could use a break to regroup before the next round.

"I don't suppose you'd leave if I told you this isn't a good time," she said at the front door of her house.

"I would if you insisted—and if you promised to rest." Jake had walked her from his truck, observing her carefully for any sign of more cramps. There'd been none, but he was still cautious, not wanting another scare. "How are you feeling?"

"Better." She fished a ring of keys from her purse and unlocked the door.

"Has this happened before?" He accompanied her inside. "The cramps, I mean."

"Last week. And with my previous pregnancies." She choked on the word.

Jake went to her, put an arm around her shoulders and led her to the living room couch, where he arranged the pillows. "Lie down. I'll get you some water."

She nodded and did as he told her.

He knew his way around Lilly's kitchen, having visited her house during the time they'd dated. Drinking glasses were kept in the cupboard to the left of the sink. He removed two and filled them with ice and water. Once that was done, he paused. Five seconds stretched into thirty, then sixty.

There was no reason not to return to Lilly. Yet somehow he couldn't bring himself to leave the kitchen. Not until he'd sorted through some of what he was feeling.

She was having a baby. *His* baby. And from what she'd told him, one who might not be born normal—if at all. Jake had fathered three daughters, and while his ex-wife, Ellen, had fretted endlessly, he hadn't given potential complications of the pregnancies more than a moment's thought.

He remembered lying in bed one night just before Briana was born, his hand on Ellen's stomach. She'd asked him if he would still love their child even if he or she was born with something wrong. He'd answered yes, giving her the reassurance she needed, never really considering the reality of "something wrong." Those kinds of tragedies happened to other people, not him.

Now he'd have to consider it.

He'd also have to decide what to do if the baby *was* born normal.

Jake pushed away from the counter and took the glasses of water to the living room. Regardless of the baby's health, he and Lilly were in this together. Possibly for the rest of their lives.

He paused at the archway leading to the living room, brought to a halt by his sudden worry. His daughters were already having trouble coping with a stepfather. How would they feel about a new sibling? One who might be born with a chromosomal abnormality.

"I'D LIKE TO GO with you to the doctor tomorrow."

Lilly braced a hand on the couch cushion and sat up straight. Surprise gave her voice an edge. "You don't have to do that. It's just a routine examination."

Jake handed her the glass of water before sitting down on the couch, which put them in close proximity. *Too* close.

"I want to. I'm the baby's father, and I have a responsibility to go with you."

"There really isn't much need at this stage." She took a sip of water and set the glass on the side table before her trembling fingers could give her away. Why hadn't she insisted he leave when they were standing outside her door?

"No need because you might lose the baby?" he asked, crossing his legs.

"Yes, that's part of it."

"Even more reason for me to be there."

She was no stranger to his stubbornness, having encountered it before. Those occasions, however, had involved the ranch or center's business, not her *personal* business.

"If your cramps return or the news isn't good," he said, "you don't want to be alone. You won't want to drive yourself home."

She reluctantly conceded that his argument had merit, and in all fairness, she couldn't refuse him. Like it or not, he had certain rights, along with duties and obligations. They'd have to decide on those, as well.

Pressing a palm to her cheek, she closed her eyes. It was too soon. Everything was happening too fast. She'd believed she'd have more time and more answers before informing Jake of her pregnancy. If only she could take back the last couple of hours…

"Are you okay?"

"Fine," she said and tried for a casual smile. "I just hate inconveniencing you."

"No problem. I can rearrange my schedule."

"Why not wait until later when I have an ultrasound?"

The instant she made the suggestion, she regretted it. Hadn't she told Dr. Paul no tests? Now she was committed. And worse, Jake would be in the exam room, viewing the monitor along with her. What if Dr. Paul found something irregular or of concern? Jake would ask questions, become involved, think he was entitled to participate in any and all decisions. Lilly wasn't sure she could handle bad news and his take-charge attitude.

God forbid he'd want her to terminate the pregnancy. He hadn't mentioned abortion so far, but maybe that was because he hadn't thought of it yet. Dr. Paul would likely bring up that option if the ultrasound indicated any…irregularities. Lilly's other doctors had.

So be it. Jake would have no more luck convincing her to end her pregnancy than her ex-husband had.

"I know about doctor visits and that they can be emotional," he said with a compassion she hadn't expected. "Remember, I have three daughters. I went with Ellen to the doctor's quite a few times."

Emotional didn't begin to describe Lilly's appointments. "Your ex-wife's pregnancies were all normal. Mine weren't."

"I'd like to talk with your doctor if I can."

She nearly fell off the couch. "About what?"

"Your genetic problems. The baby's health."

"Why?" Alarm stiffened her spine, and her face felt hot. "I'll tell you everything you need to know."

Wrong. She'd tell him only what she wanted him to hear and judging by the narrowing of his eyes, he'd guessed as much.

"What's really bothering you, Lilly? Surely your ex-husband went to the doctor with you."

Husband. Jake's question hit the nail square on the head. They weren't married. While he had rights when it came to the baby, he didn't where *she* was concerned, and she wasn't about to let him coerce her into doing something she didn't want to do, like Brad had.

"Everything's moving a little fast for me."

"For me, too."

"It's not the same." She shook her head. "For one thing, we aren't dating anymore."

"Lots of unattached couples have babies together and make it work."

"We aren't a typical couple experiencing a typical pregnancy."

"That's true," he said after a moment. "And you have every reason not to trust me. I handled our breakup badly. But I promise you I won't abandon you or this child. Regardless of...the circumstances."

Lilly huddled in the corner of the couch. Jake could be a steamroller when he made up his mind about something, and she wasn't about to let him into her life again, at least not anymore than necessary. He'd already walked out on her once when the situation between them was a whole lot less complicated. For all she knew, he might do it again, and she'd had her fill of men leaving her when the going got tough.

He reached for her hand. She hadn't realized how cold her fingers were until he wrapped them in his much warmer ones, and her instinct to pull away faded.

"What time is your appointment tomorrow?" He stroked the inside of her wrist with his thumb. It was something he'd done frequently when they were dating.

She remained mute, trying to resist the familiar sensations his touch evoked.

"Will you tell me if I promise to keep my mouth shut during the visit?"

"When have you ever done that?"

Though she'd been mostly serious, he laughed. "It won't be easy. But I'm a man of my word." He sobered, and his grip on her fingers tightened.

"True." She remembered the last promise he'd made to her. It was in this very room, on the night he broke up with her.

I won't make things any harder than they have to be b
beating around the bush.

Jake had gotten right to the point, and she'd cried for thre
days afterward. If not for the unexpected gift of an old mule
she wouldn't have spoken to him for months. Neither woul
she be facing the dilemma of what to do about her appoint
ment with Dr. Paul tomorrow.

"I'll stay in the waiting room during your exam," he said

She frowned, not quite believing him. "I thought yo
wanted to talk to my doctor."

"I'm willing to hold off until you feel more comfortable
about it." He resumed his mesmerizing stroking of her wrist

Lilly supposed that if she stood her ground, she could pu
Jake off temporarily, though not indefinitely. Payson wasn'
a large town, and there was only a handful of ob/gyns. He'd
heard her mention Dr. Paul by name. Locating her office
would be easy enough. It was even possible Ellen had gone
to Dr. Paul, too. With his stubborn streak, she wouldn't put i
past him to camp out in the parking lot until she arrived fo
an appointment and then follow her inside.

"Okay," she heard herself agreeing. "You can come, bu
only if you stay in the waiting room."

He smiled. "Deal."

No, Lilly thought. *Test.*

If he could contain his impulse to take charge and take over
if he stuck to the rules they both agreed to, then maybe they
had a chance of being successful co-parents.

"What time is your appointment?" He took out his PDA.

"One-fifteen at the Payson Physicians Plaza. Suite two
thousand and three."

"Would you like to stop for lunch on the way?"

"No, thanks." Between her morning sickness and nerves,
she doubted she'd be able to eat.

"I'll pick you up at work."

"Fine," she said, biting her lower lip and hoping she didn't regret her decision.

"So, what did the doctor say?"

Jake leaned forward, his forearms balanced on the table. He'd spoken softly, Lilly presumed, so the few nearby diners and waitresses didn't hear him.

"Everything appears normal," she answered in an equally soft voice.

"What about the cramps and bleeding?"

"She says that's not uncommon in the first trimester. A woman's body goes through a lot of changes during pregnancy, and…" Lilly tried to recall exactly how Dr. Paul had put it. "Sometimes the changes cause side effects."

"But you're okay? And the baby's okay?"

"Yes." *For now*.

She twirled her glass of milk, noticing the faint trail of condensation it left on the scratched Formica. When he'd learned she'd skipped lunch, he'd insisted on taking her to the Hilltop Café—another of his tenants in the same small complex as Horizon and his aunt's antique shop—so she could have a quick bite before returning to work. Her first instinct had been to refuse, but then she thought better of it and ordered a small chef's salad to go with her milk. Skipping meals wasn't good for the baby or her own health and as often as not, eating settled her chronic nausea.

"Is that all she said?" Jake took a bite of the key lime pie he'd ordered with his iced tea.

"I'm supposed to take it easy for the next few weeks. Not lift heavy objects and rest as much as possible."

"Why don't I arrange for someone to clean your house? I can have one of the maids from the ranch come over."

"That's not necessary." The worry of being steamrolled returned, and Lilly's defenses shot up. "I can still lift a dust cloth and push a broom."

"Okay." The staccato pinging of fork tines on his now-empty plate left no doubt that Jake would be bringing up the subject again.

Trying to look at the situation from a different perspective, Lilly supposed his constant attempts to take charge could be construed as kindness. Maybe she was overreacting, looking for ulterior motives that weren't there. After all, Jake was a businessman, used to making decisions and delegating tasks. Sometimes he carried those same traits into other areas of his life.

"Call me if you need anything."

"I will." Lilly meant what she'd said.

If she truly needed help and couldn't get it elsewhere, she'd ask Jake. While she had friends in Payson, none of them possessed Jake's resources or had as much of a stake in her welfare. Her family was in Albuquerque. She'd left them and her closest friends and acquaintances when her ex-husband's employer transferred him to their Phoenix office seven years ago. After almost five years in Phoenix and two in Payson, she hadn't connected with anyone the way she had with Jake. She'd even contemplated a future with him.

Now, it seemed, she had one. Just not the one she'd envisioned.

"I really should get back to work." She wiped her hands on her napkin and set it aside. "Thanks for lunch."

"When's your next doctor's appointment?"

"Two weeks from today. Same time. You don't have to drive me," she added with what she hoped was firm insistence.

"I'd like to, if you don't mind."

He didn't say, "And I want to come into the exam room

with you and meet your doctor," but she sensed it was on the tip of his tongue.

"All right," she said, deciding to pick her battles. Besides, having Jake along wasn't nearly the hardship she'd expected. He'd been considerate and sweet—when he wasn't trying to boss her around. Opening doors for her. Putting her at ease with small talk. Seeing to it that she ate.

"I want to be an involved father, Lilly. Before *and* after the baby is born."

"Will you still feel like that if this child has the same…birth defects as Evan?" She shuddered, remembering the horror and revulsion in her ex-husband's eyes. "Brad refused to hold Evan or even touch his tiny hand."

"I'm not like him," Jake said resolutely.

"Forgive me for not having complete faith in you. Until you've sat beside an isolette in a neonatal intensive care unit and watched your child struggle for every breath, praying he's going to survive his latest surgery and yet terrified about what kind of life he'll have if he does, you can't understand."

"No, you're right. The closest I've come to experiencing anything like that was when my sister died."

"Sorry." Lilly instantly regretted her hasty assumptions. "I'd forgotten about Hailey."

Jake's younger sister had lost her life in a riding accident several years earlier. She'd survived the fall long enough to make it to the hospital, lived long enough for her family to arrive at her bedside. Jake had told Lilly about his sister's tragic death the night they'd made love in the hot tub. The same night she'd gotten pregnant.

"She suffered such extensive brain damage that if she'd lived she wouldn't have been the same." His voice grew rough, and his gaze turned inward. "I hate to admit that after hearing the doctors' prognosis, I was almost relieved when she didn't make it. For her sake, not mine. Hailey would never have wanted to live out her life in a vegetative state, hooked up to machines and tubes that breathed and ate and went to the bathroom for her."

How well Lilly knew those machines and tubes.

Had she misjudged Jake? Been too hard on him? Was it possible that he, of all people, understood a little of what she'd been through and had a heart open enough to welcome a child like Evan?

When they were done eating, Jake paid the bill, and they left.

"You don't have to walk me to work," Lilly said outside the entrance.

He took her elbow and guided her down the walkway in front of the stores, their windows already decorated for the holidays. "It's a nice afternoon, and I can use the exercise after that pie."

Lilly smiled her first genuine smile all day. Whatever Jake did to stay fit worked like a charm. She'd seen every inch of him, skimming her fingers along the smooth ridges of his honed muscles, and knew him to be in great shape. He was one of those people who could eat ten pieces of pie every day and not gain an ounce.

"Remember, call if you need anything." They both hesitated outside the door to the center.

"Thanks. Again."

"Or if you just want to talk. You don't need a reason."

"Um, okay."

Lilly wasn't sure what to do next. Should she shake his hand? Hug him? Turn around and head to her office? He didn't leave, and the awkward minute lengthened into two.

"Daddy, Daddy!"

Jake's two youngest daughters came racing down the sidewalk, straight for him and Lilly.

"Hey, what are you doing here?" He opened his arms, and the girls flew into them.

"Mommy's dropping us off at Aunt Millie's store."

"Oh?" Jake glanced up the walkway.

So did Lilly. Her hand automatically went to her stomach, and she was infinitely glad not to be showing yet.

Jake's ex-wife exited a fire-engine red Mustang convertible and made her way toward them, heels clicking on the concrete.

"Jake. I didn't realize you'd be here." The smile she flashed Lilly was brief and disinterested. "Do you mind watching the girls for a few minutes? I was going to leave them with Millie while I did some shopping but I'm sure they'd rather stay with you."

"Not at all. I can take them home, too, if you want."

"That would be great."

"Where's Briana?"

"Some after-school function. I'll pick her up when I'm done." Ellen waved a hand before starting off. "See you later."

Lilly allowed herself to breathe again.

The girls hung on Jake's coat sleeves. "Can we go to the pet shop?" the youngest one asked. The store was a few doors down from Horizon.

"In a few minutes. Girls, do you remember Ms. Russo? You met her at the barbeque a while back." He indicated Lilly, and they nodded solemnly.

"Nice to see you again," Lilly said and winked. Jake was truly fortunate; his girls were charming.

"This is where Ms. Russo works." He pointed to the center's front door. "She's the administrator."

LeAnne examined the sign in the window, her brow furrowed in concentration, and tried to sound out the words. "The Hor-i-z-zon…"

"The Horizon Adult Day Care Center," Jake supplied.

LeAnne's eyes widened. "What's that?"

"Kind of like the summer program you and your sister go to. Only it's for grown-ups."

LeAnne and Kayla turned to each other, then burst into giggles. "Grown-ups don't need day care."

"Well, some do." Jake took the girls' hands. "Would you like to go inside and see for yourself?"

"Can we?" Kayla seemed wary but intrigued.

LeAnne, on the other hand, was reserved. "Is this where the funny people who come to the ranch are?"

"They're not funny, LeAnne."

"Yes, they are." She peered up at her father. "They make me feel weird."

Jake smiled apologetically. "Sorry…"

"Don't worry about it." Lilly wasn't offended by Le-Anne's comment. Special-needs adults could be intimidating to young children.

"Mr. Tucker!" The door to the center flew open, and Jimmy Bob landed outside, a bundle of unconstrained excitement. "I saw you through the window. Why didn't you come inside?"

Lilly stepped sideways, having experienced the force of Jimmy Bob's enthusiasm before. She needn't have bothered; she wasn't the young man's target. He rushed up to Jake and, although he was a good head shorter, enveloped him in a fierce bear hug.

"Thank you, thank you, Mr. Tucker, for Big Ben." Jimmy Bob buried his face in the front of Jake's jacket. "We love him so much."

"You're welcome." Jake awkwardly patted Jimmy Bob's back.

Lilly attempted to come to the rescue. "Jimmy Bob, you know you aren't supposed to be outside the center unless there's a staff member with you."

He stepped back from Jake, his jaw set in the determined line Lilly had come to recognize as meaning business. "*You're* a staff member."

He was, of course, right.

Georgina opened the door and sighed. "Jimmy Bob."

"I wanna stay." He hunched his shoulders.

"You can't, sweetie." Lilly took his arm. "Mr. Tucker and his daughters are leaving."

Jimmy Bob refused to budge. He'd spotted Kayla and LeAnne and stood rooted in place, grinning widely. "Hi! What's your names? Mine's Jimmy Bob. I come here almost every day."

The girls were rooted in place, too, but for different reasons, Lilly suspected. She recognized the trepidation in their small faces, LeAnne's especially. Jimmy Bob's effusiveness, though well-meaning, could be overwhelming.

"Daddy, I want to go." LeAnne yanked on her father's hand. "Now."

Kayla appeared a little less nervous than her sister but still uncertain.

"Girls," Jake reprimanded softly. "Don't be rude."

"It's all right. Let's go, Jimmy Bob." This time Lilly wasn't taking no for an answer.

"Is Briana your sister? She's my friend." Jimmy Bob ignored Lilly and leaned down to the girls' level. "Do you wanna be my friend, too?"

LeAnne cowered and backed away until she was half-hidden behind her father.

"Don't be afraid of me." Jimmy Bob's smile crumpled. "I won't hurt you." His disappointment was heart-wrenching.

"Come on, girls," Jake coaxed. "Be nice."

Lilly shook her head. "It's better if you don't force it."

"That's enough, big guy." Georgina took charge of the

situation before it worsened and pulled on one of Jimmy Bob's arms. Lilly aided by pushing on the other and together they managed to get him inside.

"I am really sorry," Jake said, gesturing at his daughters. "They're not as comfortable around the center's clients as their sister is."

"It's okay. Really." Lilly stood in the doorway, glancing over her shoulder at Jimmy Bob and Georgina. "I'll see you later," she told him, suddenly anxious to get away. "Bye, girls." She let the door close.

She went directly to her office, her earlier optimism dwindling.

Jake and his oldest daughter, Briana, might very well be capable of welcoming a child like Evan but clearly the same couldn't be said of his other girls. Not that Lilly blamed them.

Sitting at her desk, she scolded herself for her shortsightedness. She'd been so caught up in herself and Jake, she'd failed to consider the rest of his family and their reactions to a possible special-needs baby. Until today.

Chapter Six

Jake's personal assistant, Alice, poked her head around the corner of his office door. "Your cousin Carolina is here. She wants to know if you have a few minutes for her."

"Sure. I'm expecting a call from Howard," he said, referring to the family trust attorney. "Go ahead and put him through when he phones."

Alice retreated and a moment later, Carolina breezed into the office.

"Hey." She sat in one of the visitor's chairs, reaching for a candy from the dish Jake kept on his desk. Tall, slim and with the trademark Tucker hazel eyes, she was the envy of her three sisters because of her ability to eat whatever she wanted and never have it show.

"What's going on?" Jake took a break from the maintenance reports he'd been reviewing and leaned back in his chair.

"I just came from the kitchen. Mom asked me to drop by."

"What's wrong?" Her mother, Jake's aunt, was also the ranch's wedding coordinator and worked closely with the kitchen staff.

"Nothing we weren't expecting. Eventually." Carolina shrugged. "Olivia's retiring."

"She's threatened that before."

"This time she's serious. Her husband gave his notice at the plant. Says they're boarding up the house and taking a three-month vacation to visit their kids in El Paso and Austin, even if he has to hog-tie her to the front seat of their motor home."

"I see."

Bear Creek Ranch's kitchen manager had been employed by the Tuckers since Jake was in the third grade. All during his teens, he'd rotated at different jobs, learning the family business from the ground up. Olivia had supervised him during his stint as a dishwasher and cook's helper. He might have been the owner's son, but she'd cut him no slack, instilling in him a work ethic he didn't appreciate until he was much older and had taken over the management of Bear Creek Ranch from his father.

"What are you going to do about it?" Carolina asked. "Olivia practically runs that dining hall single-handed."

"There's nothing I can do. She's been talking about retiring for months." In hindsight, he should have started the recruitment process by now. Lilly's pregnancy had distracted him—from that and a lot of other things.

"You don't seem too broken up about this."

"I'll miss Olivia, of course. We all will. But I'm sure there's a qualified candidate out there."

"You'd better act fast. Olivia's husband's giving her until the end of January. That's just weeks away."

Carolina was the only person, besides his parents and Aunt Millie, who could order Jake around. If any of his employees or other family members so much as tried, they'd either be out of a job or put soundly in their place. Carolina was an exception because she'd filled the void left after his sister's death.

"I'll get Alice right on it." Jake didn't make a move to pick up the intercom.

Carolina studied him critically. "You care to tell me what's really bothering you? Or would you rather go on pretending that everything's fine?"

"Everything is fine."

"Please." His cousin sent him her I'm-not-buying-what-you're-selling look. "You've been out of sorts for two or three weeks now, and I'm starting to worry."

He thought for a moment and nodded. It was time he confided in someone about Lilly's pregnancy. Keeping everything inside was ruining his appetite, his sleep at night and his concentration. He didn't always appreciate Carolina's strong opinions, and they'd certainly had their share of disagreements, but she could also be a good listener, and he needed that right now.

"How much time do you have?"

"I'm going out, but not until later."

"A date?"

Carolina smiled coyly.

"Anyone I know?"

"Kevin Ward from the station."

Like most of the family, Carolina divided her days between the ranch and an outside job. She worked part-time as a roving reporter for Payson's second largest radio station, having landed the job seven months earlier when the station conducted a live broadcast from the ranch.

"Isn't he a little old for you?"

"He's forty-seven," she said with the air of someone who regularly dated men ten years her junior and twenty years her senior. "Why? What difference does it make?"

"None, as long as you're happy."

Jake had given up on his social-butterfly cousin years ago. In that regard, they were polar opposites. Carolina loved the single life, while he'd married young and begun having children almost immediately. Had Ellen not strayed, he'd probably still be married.

And Lilly wouldn't be pregnant now. At least not with his child.

A surge of excitement halted him in his tracks. He was going to be a father again. Jake had been so wrapped up in the complications of Lilly's pregnancy and their relationship—past and present—he'd forgotten about the thrill of impending fatherhood. In that instant, his perspective, along with his attitude, changed.

"You okay?" Carolina asked.

"Yeah. I just remembered something."

"Must've been important. You were seriously gone for a minute there."

He smiled. "It was important."

Carolina snatched another candy from the dish. "So, is it woman troubles that have you down?"

"What makes you say that?"

She laughed good-naturedly. "Let's face it, Jake, you're surrounded by them. Three daughters, an ex-wife, a mother, an aunt and four cousins," she ended, including herself and her three sisters. "I don't know how you and your dad stand it."

"We've developed a high tolerance," he answered jokingly.

"The only thing you don't have is a girlfriend—well, you did, but you blew it."

He didn't respond.

"Wait a minute." She put down the partially unwrapped candy. "Did something happen that I don't know about?"

Jake inhaled deeply before speaking. "Lilly's pregnant."

"Wow!" Carolina's mouth hung open for a good five seconds. "You're not kidding."

"No, I'm not. She's about twelve weeks along. I've known for the last three."

"I guess that explains your recent mood."

"Sorry to be so irritable."

"Why haven't you said anything?" Carolina still looked shocked.

"Two reasons. Lilly isn't ready to make an announcement. So, no talking to anyone." He leveled a warning finger at her. "And I didn't want the girls to find out. Not until I was ready to tell them. They're already dealing with so much, what with the divorce and Ellen getting married next month." Briana had informed him recently in no uncertain terms that she refused to be her mother's maid of honor.

"Are you okay with being a dad again?"

"Sure."

"Is that hesitation I hear in your voice?"

Jake explained about Lilly's previous pregnancies, her son, Evan, and the end of her marriage.

"Wow!" Carolina repeated, then picked up the candy and popped it in her mouth. "The hell with my date tonight."

"Hey, don't cancel on my account."

"Trust me, this is more important." For several minutes, Jake answered her questions. When they were done, she asked, "Can I be honest without you getting offended?"

"When aren't you honest?"

"This is serious."

"All right." He sobered.

She paused, then proceeded cautiously. "Losing the baby would be hard. I'm not minimizing that, so please don't take this the wrong way."

"I'll try." He was starting to worry.

"But have you really considered the ramifications of having a severely handicapped child?"

"Well…I admit my knowledge is limited."

"It won't be easy."

"I was thinking about Grandpa Walter the other day and everything we had to go through with him. We managed, didn't we?"

"Oh, Jake. You can't compare taking care of him to taking care of a gravely ill child who depends on machines to survive. Lilly's husband couldn't deal with it, and they were in love."

"I have…feelings for her."

"You dated for six weeks. They were *married*."

Jake remained silent. He hated it when his cousin found the holes in his arguments.

"The pressure is incredible," she went on. "You just told me her husband could hardly bring himself to hold his own child. Will you be different?"

"Yes!"

"What about your girls?"

He remembered that day at the center when Jimmy Bob had tried to make friends with Kayla and LeAnne and what a disaster that had been. Doubts crept in, and he pushed away from his desk. He'd have to work harder at convincing his youngest daughters that people with special needs were no different than everyone else.

"Sorry to upset you," Carolina said.

"It's okay. I need to face reality."

She shook her head. "Your parents will freak when you tell them."

Jake had been concentrating on his daughters and not his parents. He rubbed the back of his neck, the muscles there taut and aching.

"Is there anything I can do to help?"

"Thanks. I'll let you know if and when. Lilly and I need to make some decisions before I say anything."

"Not that I'm any kind of expert in these matters, but I don't think you should wait too long."

"I agree, but it's been hard pinning her down." He thought about their appointment at Dr. Paul's office last week, his second time accompanying Lilly. "She dodges every question I ask about the baby or our future together and insists on doing nothing until she's a lot farther along."

"I don't blame her," Carolina said. "From what you've told me, her pregnancy hasn't been easy so far. She must be afraid of losing the baby."

"And afraid I'll abandon her."

"You wouldn't do that!"

"I did once before."

"You broke up. That happens to couples. And you didn't know she was pregnant."

"She doesn't trust me to stick with her for the long haul. Especially if the baby's born with the same birth defects as the others."

"What about tests? Can't the doctors predict these things?"

"She mentioned having an ultrasound later on."

"Maybe you'll get some answers then."

"I hope so." Jake did want answers and prayed the news would be good.

"What about health insurance? Our group plan has restrictions."

"Good question." And another concern to add to Jake's growing list. He could wind up paying sizeable out-of-pocket expenses, though it was a responsibility he was more than willing to assume. "Lilly probably has insurance, too, through the center. I'll have to figure out how to ask her without making her defensive."

Carolina's expression softened. "I'm sure everything will be fine. How can it not be with you as the dad?"

He smiled. "There are times I'm kind of excited about being a dad again."

"And who knows? You could have a son."

"Yeah." His smile widened.

He was about to suggest Carolina leave to get ready for her date when his intercom buzzed.

"That's Howard. I've been expecting his call." He picked up the receiver. "Yes, Alice."

"Lilly Russo just called. She said to tell you she's at the hospital emergency room and needs you to come right away."

Jake bolted out from behind his desk, grabbing his keys from the credenza on his way to the door.

"What's wrong?" Carolina chased after him.

"Alice will tell you."

He ran to the parking lot and climbed into the closest vehicle, which happened to be one of the old maintenance trucks, and drove it straight through to Payson without stopping.

LILLY GAVE A start when the privacy curtain surrounding her hospital gurney was swept aside. Jake entered the small treatment area where she'd spent the last twenty-five minutes, supposedly resting but in reality going slowly crazy. She'd spent nearly as long in the waiting room out front and then again at the counter being admitted.

"You came," she blurted, fighting to contain her emotions.

"Are you okay?" He grabbed her hands, wrapping his strong fingers around them.

"Better." She laid her head back and closed her eyes. "The cramps have stopped, and the bleeding's a lot lighter."

"Bleeding? Has that happened before?"

"Yes, with all my previous pregnancies."

Hospital emergency rooms were scary and uncomfortable. The relief Lilly felt at seeing Jake was enormous. And disconcerting. He was competent and capable and exuded confidence. She supposed it was natural for her to rely on him and to call him first in this crisis. Most of his family and employees would do the same. But she didn't want to be like them, accepting his help and his presence in her life without question.

Not yet.

He bent to kiss the top of her head. Her eyes flew open and a sob escaped her lips. Embarrassed at her outburst, she turned her head.

"Shh." He pushed a lock of hair from her face. "Everything's going to be fine."

"I wish I knew that for sure."

Lilly had contacted the ranch looking for Jake in a moment of pure terror, when the cramps and bleeding were at their worst. Once the danger seemed to have passed, she began to regret her impulsiveness. Jake had a history of running scared when she made assumptions about their relationship and placed too many expectations on him.

She'd seriously contemplated retrieving her cell phone from her purse to call him back. She might have done it, too, if not for the strict instructions she'd been given to lie still and not strain herself. But now that Jake was here, comforting and reassuring her with warm, soft strokes of his fingertips, she was glad she'd phoned him in the first place, glad to have someone with her.

"What did Dr. Paul say?" He pulled a metal chair closer to the gurney and sat down. "Has she been in to see you?"

"Not yet. She's on her way. A lab technician came by a little while ago and drew blood." Her glance traveled to the bandage on the inside of her elbow, and she slipped her arm underneath the blanket. Why were emergency rooms always so damn cold?

"Hi, there."

The same friendly nurse who'd attended to Lilly earlier

appeared from behind the curtain. She'd asked a hundred questions during the brief exam. Questions like, when did the cramps start? How severe were they? Do you feel dizzy or faint?

And the worst one of all, have you previously miscarried or lost a baby?

But the question the nurse asked now was even more disconcerting. "Are you ready to take a ride?"

"Where to?" Lilly attempted to sit up.

Jake restrained her by laying a hand on her arm.

"Down the hall a bit," the nurse said. "Your doctor just arrived, and she's ordered an ultrasound." The nurse dropped the clipboard she'd been carrying onto the gurney by Lilly's feet and raised the side rails. Straightening, she showered Jake with a thousand-watt smile. "Is this your husband?"

"Ah...no."

"I'm the baby's father," Jake said, standing.

"Then you'll want to come along." The nurse flipped a lever to release the brake.

Lilly fought an overpowering sense of disorientation and loss of control. Everything was moving so fast. Again. She didn't want any tests and had told Dr. Paul as much. Now, it seemed she was having one and Jake would be accompanying her. He might suggest terminating the pregnancy if the results indicated an abnormality, and she couldn't do that. Nor did she want to go through another pregnancy like her second, knowing all along her baby's chances of surviving were nil. Some might say that wasn't a very realistic attitude, but hope was the only thing that kept her going.

"Where's Dr. Paul? I need to talk to her first," Lilly protested when the nurse positioned herself behind the gurney and began to push.

"She's signing the necessary paperwork and will be here in a minute."

Lilly remembered the last series of ultrasounds she'd undergone and the images that had appeared on the screen. She could still hear the "tap-tap" of the doctor's pencil as he pointed out the deformities to her and her ex-husband, Brad. Seeing similar images again today, learning the baby wasn't normal and might not survive, would devastate her.

No telling what it would do to Jake.

"Wait!"

"I know you're afraid. But I'm here with you." His voice, so close to her ear, was soothing, as if he could make everything okay just by saying so.

"What if the ultrasound shows…" She couldn't say the word.

"What if it doesn't?"

"I realize I'm being unreasonable but I don't want to… can't go through what I did before. I don't want to know that I'm carrying a damaged baby. I need to have hope."

"An ultrasound can give you that hope."

"It can also destroy it."

"Whatever it shows, we're in this together, Lilly."

Oddly enough, his reassurances worked, and she felt calmed. He walked beside her down the hall. Lilly's ex-husband hadn't done that. Neither had he shielded her from the too-bright fluorescent lights, or touched her arm to let her know she wasn't alone in this ordeal. She'd needed Brad to be there. To share her misery and grief. To pray for a miracle. To lend his shoulder to cry on when the doctor delivered the dismal prognosis. Instead, he'd withdrawn and borne his suffering all by himself, leaving her to do the same.

She observed Jake through lowered lids. He looked fearless and strong—like he could cope with whatever came next.

Little did he know. He'd fathered three healthy children and had no idea what could be waiting for them on the other side of the door.

Chapter Seven

It seemed the moment they entered the ultrasound room, everything moved at superspeed. The nurse prepped Lilly for the procedure, chatting constantly, mostly with Jake. Lilly's cheeks flamed when the nurse lowered her blanket and arranged her gown. Her embarrassment mystified and annoyed her. Jake had seen her wearing far less and had let her know with softly murmured words and exquisite touches how much he liked and appreciated her naked form.

When the nurse turned her back, Lilly tugged at the hem of her gown. The extra inch or two of modesty eased a bit of her tension but not for long. Her anxiety went through the roof when the door opened and Dr. Paul entered, her street clothes visible beneath a lab coat and those funny little paper slippers covering her shoes. She greeted Lilly and reached for the clipboard the nurse had set on the counter.

"I'm guessing you're the baby's father," Dr. Paul said to Jake while flipping pages.

"Yes, ma'am."

She nodded, her lips pursed in concentration. "How are you doing, Lilly?" She handed the clipboard to the nurse, who dimmed the overhead lights, and then faded into a corner.

Jake stood by Lilly's left shoulder, his position giving him an unobstructed view of the monitor screen.

"I'm doing much better," she told Dr. Paul. "The bleeding and cramps have stopped. There's probably no need for an ultrasound."

Dr. Paul lifted the blanket covering Lilly's lower half. Though the exam was conducted discreetly and efficiently, she suffered another bout of acute embarrassment. She didn't relax until Dr. Paul pulled the blanket back into place.

"I understand your concerns, Lilly, but we really should see what's going on with you. If only to rule out certain things like ectopic pregnancy."

Everything Dr. Paul said made sense, and Lilly was certain it was in her own and the baby's best interest. Her heart, however, still hadn't healed from her previous losses and cried out, "Not yet."

Jake's touch, soft and gentle on her shoulder, lent her courage.

"Nothing invasive," she insisted. "I won't risk a miscarriage."

"We'll use an abdominal probe. I will, however, ask you to reconsider if the test shows anything out of the ordinary."

Lilly involuntarily gasped when Dr. Paul applied a lubricating gel to her abdomen. The nurse turned on the ultrasound machine, and the screen came to life.

"This might feel a little cold." Dr. Paul delivered the warning a mere second before the probe came to rest on the tiny rise of Lilly's exposed belly.

She tensed, every muscle in her body turning to stone. As much as she dreaded hearing bad news, she couldn't take her eyes off the screen. A swirling black, white and gray image appeared. Dr. Paul moved the probe, and the image gradually came into focus.

"There we go," she said, her tone warm and a little excited. "Mom and Dad, say hello to your baby."

Lilly paid strict attention to every nuance in her doctor's voice, listening for the tiniest hint of something wrong. There was none.

"See here." Dr. Paul indicated a small pulsating shape in the center of the screen. "We have a nice, strong heartbeat."

Lilly repeated the words in her head. They seemed almost too wonderful to be true.

Dr. Paul went on to point out the baby's head, feet, spine, lungs and even a small face. Lilly's breath caught at the sight, and her chest ached with indescribable longing.

"Measurements are good, well within normal range." Dr. Paul continued to move the probe.

"Can you see what sex the baby is?" Jake asked.

"Don't tell us," Lilly said in a rush. It was enough to know the baby was growing normally.

"I can't tell anyway." Dr. Paul squinted at the image. "The umbilical cord's in the way."

"So, everything's fine?"

The hope in Jake's voice echoed Lilly's. She marveled at their shared anticipation and how natural and right it felt. They were two expectant parents, enjoying their first baby pictures.

"Well." Dr. Paul's tone changed to one of caution. "I can't say with complete certainty that everything's fine or that your baby is perfectly healthy. Many problems aren't detectable with a simple ultrasound, especially at this stage."

How well Lilly knew that. Her first child's ultrasound had shown nothing of concern, and her pregnancy had been relatively trouble-free for the first couple of months.

Before her mood could sink lower, Dr. Paul offered reassurances. "But I can tell you this baby is thriving and looks normal for a twelve- to thirteen-week-old fetus."

Tears leaked from the sides of Lilly's eyes. Christmas was almost a month away, but she felt like she'd gotten her first present. Maybe now she could tell her parents about the baby when they came for the holidays.

Jake reached for her hand, and she grabbed it, grateful for his strength.

Dr. Paul's faint smile disappeared. "To be absolutely sure, we could perform additional tests. When you come in for your next appointment—"

"No more tests. Not yet."

"Don't you think we ought to hear what your doctor has to say?" Jake asked softly.

"I need something positive to hold on to if I'm going to make it through the months ahead. You've given me that today," she told the doctor.

"We could have more positive news," Jake said.

"I want to hold off. Please. Just a little while longer. I promise to reconsider if I have more…incidents."

"Okay."

"What?"

"I said okay. If you're willing to take the chance, so am I."

"Really?" She tilted her head to get a better look at him.

He smiled encouragingly. "You and I are going to make a beautiful baby together. I don't see how anything else is possible."

Lilly stared at Jake, searching for any indication of insincerity. The face gazing down at her was open and honest and full of joy, the same kind of joy that burst inside her during those rare moments when she wasn't worrying herself sick.

"We're almost finished," Dr. Paul said, distracting Lilly and returning her to the present. She advised her on what to do when she got home and until her next visit. "Call if you start bleeding and cramping again." After making final notations on the chart, Dr. Paul told Lilly she could go home. "I don't want you driving, though."

"I'll take her," Jake said.

"What about my car? I can't leave it here."

"I'll arrange for someone from the center to drive it home for you." He let go of Lilly's hand only because the nurse needed him to move.

She wondered if he'd hold her hand again when they started down the hall and was a little disappointed that he didn't. He waited outside the treatment area so the nurse could help Lilly dress in private, but he was standing right there as soon as she stepped around the curtain. When his palm came to rest lightly on the small of her back, she said nothing, although she felt quite capable of walking on her own. She could probably walk all the way home, she realized with a surge of happiness.

We have a nice, strong heartbeat.

Dr. Paul's voice resounded in her head. Making it even better, Jake had stood by her, agreeing with her decision to decline further tests. It had been a long time since she'd left a doctor's office or medical facility in such high spirits.

She touched her belly, wishing—imagining—she could feel the heartbeat she'd viewed on the monitor. Maybe this time things would be different, and she'd be blessed with a healthy child.

Jake pressed the elevator button. She observed him as they rode down to the ground floor. If she did get her wish, she'd be faced with deciding just how much to let this man into her life.

"Over here," he said once they were outside. He led her to an older-model pickup parked crookedly and illegally in a tow-away zone.

She stopped and stared. "What happened to your truck?"

"I was in a hurry, and this one was available."

"I can't believe the police didn't give you a ticket," she said, inspecting the windshield when they got closer.

"If they did, it'd be worth every penny."

Lilly paused. That was one of the nicest things Jake had ever said to her. "Thanks for coming today. I'm glad you did."

He opened the passenger-side door for her. "I'm glad you called me."

She considered for a few seconds, then came to a decision that wasn't nearly as hard as she'd thought it would be. "Next week at my regular appointment with Dr. Paul, you can come with me into the exam room."

"You sure?"

"So long as you behave." She smiled and in a teasing tone added, "No getting bossy and taking charge on me."

"I don't do that."

"Yeah, right," she said then let out a "hmm" when it became evident she couldn't climb into the truck without a stepping stool. Not if she was obeying the doctor's orders to avoid strain.

"We might have to take my car. I'm not sure I can get in."

"No problem." He stooped as if to lift her into his arms.

"Wait!" she squeaked and stopped him with a raised hand.

He straightened, effectively trapping her between the truck seat and the hard, unyielding length of his body.

She discovered she'd wrapped her arms around his neck, where, against her better judgment, they lingered. Their eyes locked, and though she knew she should remove her arms and scoot away—if that was even possible—she didn't.

Holding Jake wasn't just for old times' sake. She truly cared for him—more than he cared for her—which was one of the main causes of their breakup.

Not that her feelings for him weren't reciprocated. There was no mistaking the tenderness shining in his hazel eyes or the sexy half-smile that both charmed and irritated her. She caught herself staring at his mouth, which was so close that kissing him would be a simple matter of rising onto her tiptoes.

Lilly resisted. It would be sheer madness. The emotional highs and lows of the last three hours had left her vulnerable and she was confusing Jake's attentiveness with affection. Or something stronger. Thank goodness sanity returned. Before she could completely withdraw her arms, he clasped her by the waist and pulled her toward him. She held the sides of his face, thinking she'd put a halt to his intentions. But the keep-your-distance tactic became a loving caress as her thumbs brushed the faint stubble shadowing his jaw.

His hands slipped inside her jacket and glided up her rib cage, stopping just below her breasts, which were pressed against the confines of her bra. Breasts that were fuller than the last time she and Jake had been intimate.

"Jake." The stern objection she'd planned to deliver came out sounding like an invitation.

One he accepted.

The instant their lips touched, Lilly surrendered to him. The arms she'd almost removed tightened around his neck, and she opened her mouth, encouraging him to deepen their kiss with low, throaty moans. Jake obliged, and the passion she'd never truly lost during the months since their breakup flared to life and burned brightly.

This was unquestionably a mistake and something she'd regret later. But for now Jake's strong fingers kneading her skin though her shirt, his tongue and lips tantalizing, were exactly the emotional balm she needed, and she took every ounce of comfort he was willing to give.

The blazing intensity of their kiss lasted several minutes longer, then slowly began to ebb. Their mouths drew apart but their embrace continued. He seemed to sense that she needed more time before he let go. Sliding her hands to his shoulders, she waited for her breathing to calm.

But at his next words, her breathing stopped completely, and her hands fell limp at her sides.

"Marry me, Lilly."

"I CAN'T MARRY YOU, Jake! Not now."

"It doesn't have to be right away. We can wait a few months."

He hadn't expected Lilly to squeal with delight at his spontaneous proposal but neither had he anticipated the absolute horror on her face or the tears filling her eyes. Lots of couples married because of a pregnancy. Surely she'd expected him to propose eventually, or at least bring up the subject of marriage. He'd certainly been considering it since she'd told him about the baby.

She raised her hands to her lips. "Sorry. I didn't mean to overreact. I'm just so surprised."

Okay, he was wrong. She hadn't thought about marrying him. Jake didn't know whether to be hurt or amused.

He took a step back and rested his hand on the passenger door, deciding to be philosophical. His timing was off. Lilly'd had a difficult day and was clearly drained. He shouldn't have sprung any unplanned announcements on her, much less propose. His retreat came to a grinding halt when she abruptly burst into sobs.

"Hey, what's wrong?" He moved closer and put an arm around her. "Don't cry, sweetheart. Everything's going to work out fine."

Jake was prepared for her to push him away. But she didn't, and instead nestled her face in the crook of his neck, her sobs so wrenching she shook from head to toe. He let her cry, glad that she was turning to him, and rubbed her back. Eventually, she quieted but made no effort to move. He liked holding Lilly, so he said nothing for several minutes.

"Let's get in the truck," he suggested softly when she seemed ready.

She released him and wiped her cheeks. He helped her climb into the cab, then went around to the driver's side and got in, too.

"I feel so stupid," she said when he shut his door.

"Don't. This is a hospital parking lot." Rather than start the truck, he set the keys on the dash. "Crying people are pretty common. Marriage proposals, probably not so common," he added wryly.

"I really botched that, didn't I?"

The truck was an older model, so it had a bench seat, and Lilly could sit near the middle with her legs angled toward Jake. He took a chance and put an arm across the seat back. She didn't recoil. But she didn't lean in to him as she had before, either.

"I botched it more. The next time I ask you to marry me, I'll do it right. Ring, flowers, down on one knee."

"Oh, Jake."

He thought for a second she might start crying again. When she didn't, he blundered on, hoping to get past the awkward moment and onto some meaningful conversation.

"I'd like us to be married when the baby's born. Is that so wrong?"

"No, if anything, it's sweet." She sighed. "And under different circumstances, I'd probably want the same thing."

"Different? Meaning…what?" he asked when she didn't elaborate.

"I already had one marriage fall apart under the stress of a child with special needs. I don't want to go through that twice."

"You're not going to lose this baby, and I'm not like your ex-husband." He cut her off before she could disagree. "Okay, I know you have plenty of reason to doubt me."

"You did break up with me."

"This is different."

"How can I be sure?"

"You could be sure if we were married."

"That didn't stop Brad from leaving." She tried to smile but failed miserably. "Everything is so damn complicated."

"The only way to uncomplicate it is to talk to me." The truck cab was beginning to warm up. He would have taken off his jacket but he didn't want to remove his arm from the back of the seat.

"We have to be realistic," she said. "The reasons you ended our relationship haven't changed. Your daughters are still upset about Ellen remarrying, still hate the idea of a stepfather. You can't possibly think they'll be happier about me and our baby."

"They'll come around sooner or later."

"You didn't believe that two months ago. Something tells me you still don't. And what about LeAnne?"

"What about her?"

"She was scared to death of Jimmy Bob that day at the center. How do you think she'd react to a new sibling who's born with birth defects?"

"You saw the ultrasound. This baby's going to be fine."

"Which doesn't change the fact that your daughters will be furious with you. It's not a good way to start a marriage, is it?"

Ellen was doing just that, but the thought didn't console Jake. Briana and her mother were hardly speaking. He didn't want the same thing to happen with him.

"I really didn't plan on having another baby," Lilly said haltingly.

"I know that."

"I was on the pill."

He nodded. "I know that, too."

"You had sex with me believing I was protected. And I *was*…or I was *supposed* to be, anyway. Only I wound up pregnant. You're a decent guy, Jake. You probably think it's your duty to marry me."

"I do feel responsible. But I should. You didn't get pregnant alone."

"You're missing the point." She struggled visibly for control. "I won't trap you in a relationship with me. That wasn't the deal. And I'd never forgive myself if I came between you and your girls."

Jake scowled. "Is that why you think I'm here? Because you trapped me?"

"I'm worried that's how you feel."

"Believe me, I don't."

"Maybe not today. Tomorrow could be another story."

"Did your ex-husband accuse you of trapping him?"

Pain flashed in her eyes. "He made it clear when he left that my inability to give him healthy children was a big factor in the divorce."

"He's a jerk." Jake had another word for Lilly's ex but refrained from saying it out loud. "There are other options for couples in your situation."

"Adoption was out. He wanted a biological child."

"He must have had a giant ego."

"Be honest. Most men want their children to be their biological offspring."

"Not all."

"This coming from a man with three daughters."

Jake didn't dispute her. Ellen had gotten pregnant so easily, and their three girls had been born without a single complication. If he was honest, he'd admit he couldn't understand what Lilly's ex-husband had been through or why he felt the way he did. He could only see how much the man had hurt her.

"Doctors can do some pretty incredible things nowadays," he said.

"That's true. And in vitro fertilization using donor eggs might have been an option if we'd had the money. After Evan, our finances were wiped out." She leaned back in the truck seat, her posture defeated. "I think it was easier for Brad to divorce me and find a woman with normal DNA than wait until we could pay off our bills and save more money."

"He remarried?"

"Six months after the papers were finalized. He and his new wife had a baby a year later. I understand from mutual friends that she's expecting again."

"Jeez, Lilly."

"I won't pretend I'm not bothered by it."

"You wouldn't be human if you weren't."

"I'm happy for him. Really." She turned and offered Jake a watery smile. "I just want some of that same happiness for myself."

"You'll have it." He lowered his arm and squeezed her shoulders. "If you find yourself doubting it, remember the ultrasound."

"That was wonderful." Her smile widened.

Jake wanted to kiss her even more in that moment than he had earlier and almost surrendered to temptation. But a white coupe with "Security" painted on the side pulled even with the truck, crushing his impulse. The uniformed man inside beeped his horn.

"It appears my luck's run out," Jake said.

"I'm surprised it lasted this long." Lilly slid over toward the door and fastened her seat belt.

He half wished she'd slid closer to him. The ride to her place would be considerably more enjoyable with her snuggled beside him.

"Look, I jumped the gun with my proposal earlier." He eased the truck onto the road and into Payson's small-town version of rush-hour traffic. Dusk had settled and lights everywhere were coming on. "But I want you to know I was sincere."

"I'm touched. Really."

Lilly laid her head back. Only then did Jake notice the fatigue marring her lovely features. She must not be sleeping well, which wasn't good for her or the baby. He wished there was more he could do for her. He wished she'd *let* him do more. So far, she'd stuck to her decision and refused his assistance. Until today…

Maybe he was making progress after all.

"I can't saddle you with a sick child," she said, a hitch in her voice. "That's not fair and not what you bargained for when we got involved."

"You wouldn't be saddling me. I want our child to have my name, and I want you to have the assurance that I'll be a responsible and committed parent." The intensity of his words gave him pause. He was certainly a different man from the one who'd run fast and hard a few months ago. Was the baby responsible? More likely the baby's mother and his changing feelings toward her.

They'd reached her house, which was located in one of the newer developments that had been built during a recent economic boom. Jake turned into her driveway and cut the engine. Lilly immediately opened her door. So much for sitting and talking a while longer.

"Will you at least *consider* marrying me?" They stopped on her front step. She didn't invite him inside, and he tried not to read more into that than was there.

"I won't dismiss the idea entirely. That's the best I can offer."

He hated settling; he was a man who went after what he wanted and didn't quit until he got it.

"Have dinner with me Friday night?"

"I…" She shoved her hands in her coat pockets and hunched her shoulders against the cool evening air.

"Hear me out before you say no." Jake knew he had only this one chance to sway Lilly's opinion regarding them. She was on home ground and retreating more and more by the second—physically and emotionally. "I think we should see each other twice a week. Socially. Doctor and hospital visits don't count."

"You want to...date?"

"We're having a baby. Like it or not, we'll be seeing quite a bit of each other for a long time to come." He'd rather it was across his breakfast table every morning, but she'd rejected his proposal. "Don't you agree we'll be better parents if we're on good terms?"

"Of course. But dating?"

"Think of it as two friends hanging out."

She sent him a mistrustful look.

"We can shop for maternity clothes and baby furniture. Go to yoga class. Drink herbal tea while I listen to you complain about your water retention. Whatever friends do."

That earned him a chuckle.

But she quickly sobered and asked, "No pressure? Strictly social? I can't handle it if you're popping the question every time we go out."

He placed a hand over his heart. "Scout's honor."

"I suppose we could try." The crack in the wall she'd erected widened. "See how it goes."

Her enthusiasm left a lot to be desired but Jake took what he could get. "Good. How about I pick you up at seven on Friday?"

"Why do I think you have another agenda?"

Because he did—that of further exploring their renewed and deepening relationship.

He could understand Lilly's rejection of his proposal; she wouldn't act impulsively where her child was concerned. His goal was to take the necessary steps to help his daughters adjust to a blended family and to make sure Lilly's decision to marry him was well thought-out and deliberate. That it was a decision she'd never regret.

And if he had to woo her one dinner date, one yoga class, one shopping spree at a time, he'd do it gladly.

Chapter Eight

Lilly emerged from the restroom stall and went directly to the sink. After washing her hands, she automatically checked her blouse and tugged it into place. The strategic folds hid her gently rounded belly but wouldn't for much longer, not at seventeen weeks pregnant. She couldn't believe how fast the weeks had flown by and that it was January already. Any day now she'd have to start telling people—apart from the handful she already had. And *they'd* learned only after she'd gone a full three weeks without any spotting or cramps.

Her parents had expressed mixed emotions. They knew how much Lilly wanted children but were understandably concerned about her ability to endure the loss of a fourth child. And though they'd wisely said little, they were also unhappy about her unmarried state. To her relief, Jake hadn't mentioned his proposal when he'd come over Christmas Eve for dinner and to meet her parents. Lilly had hoped he might bring his daughters, too, so that she could get to know them better. But he hadn't, probably because she was starting to show. Nor had he told them about the baby yet.

Lilly's boss and his wife had been next on her list of people to tell. After explaining her circumstances, they'd agreed not to say anything to the staff until Lilly was ready.

She cradled her middle and whispered a soft prayer for the life growing inside her. The baby who'd first turned her world upside down now completed it. Granted, she spent half her day anxious and agitated, but the other half was spent imagining herself holding a healthy, beautiful baby. Could Dr. Paul be right? Would a different father, a different DNA combination, make the difference?

Jake seemed to think so.

Keeping to their agreement, they'd gone out twice a week for the past five weeks, and it wasn't the hardship Lilly had expected. He took her to dinner a lot, which accounted for some of her recent weight gain. But they also went on day trips, like a hike through the easy trails at the ranch or renting a paddle boat at nearby Commodore Lake—with Jake doing most of the paddling.

They had fun together, but then, they'd had fun before their breakup, too. Their instant and natural camaraderie had been what attracted her to him in the first place. Jake was helping to take the pressure off their new relationship by not bringing up the *M* word again, although she doubted that would last.

Truth be told, she'd entertained the idea of marrying him once or twice. Okay, three or four times…a week. Her reasons to wait still outnumbered her reasons to accept his proposal. If her pregnancy continued to progress well and their relationship strengthened, that might not be the case in another few months.

The door to the restroom banged open, and Miranda walked in. Her face lit up at seeing Lilly, and rather than go into a stall, she joined Lilly at the sink.

"Whatcha doing?"

"Making myself presentable." Lilly smoothed at her hair, hoping Miranda didn't see through her ruse.

"There's a piece sticking up in the back."

Lilly stood immobile while Miranda patted down the fly-away strands.

Miranda held a special place in Lilly's heart because her case was so tragic. When she was two years old, she'd fallen six feet onto concrete. Broken bones weren't the worst of her injuries; she'd suffered a three-inch fracture in her skull that had left her mildly mentally disabled.

"Thank you," Lilly said when Miranda was done.

She grinned. Like a lot of the center's clients, she enjoyed being helpful. "I fix my sister's hair a lot."

"That's nice."

Miranda leaned over the sink until her face was only inches from the mirror and inspected her teeth.

"When your baby's born, can I watch it for you?"

Lilly went stone still except for her heart, which jumped inside her chest. "What makes you think I'm having a baby?" she asked haltingly.

"You're getting fat. My sister got fat, too." Miranda spun around and patted her own pudgy tummy.

Lilly hid her mortification by returning to the sink and flipping on the cold water faucet. If Miranda had noticed her condition, others must have, too. What a fool she'd been to believe she was successfully camouflaging her pregnancy with loose-fitting clothes and bulky sweaters.

"Did I say something wrong?" Miranda asked, her smile faltering.

"No, not at all." Lilly stalled by washing her hands again. She couldn't leave the restroom, not until she'd composed herself and convinced Miranda to keep her secret. The young woman was a notorious blabbermouth.

"Aren't you happy about the baby?"

Anyone who thought special-needs individuals weren't observant had another thing coming.

"Of course I'm happy. I just wasn't ready to tell people yet."

"Why not?"

"The baby might be sick." *Might not live.*

Miranda gawked at Lilly's stomach. "How can you tell when it's still inside you?"

"I had problems before."

"Sick how? Like strep throat? I had that once."

"No, not like strep throat. More serious." Lilly couldn't bring herself to be upset with Miranda. She was just trying to understand. "Sick isn't the right word. The baby could have physical problems and not..." How to say it without hurting Miranda's feelings? "Not be able to walk or talk."

"Like me." Miranda held out her foot, the one with the specially constructed shoe to compensate for her fibula, which was three inches too short. "My leg's messed up, and I don't talk real good."

"You talk fine." Too much sometimes, Lilly wryly thought. She realized that if she didn't return to her office soon, one of the staff was bound to come looking for her. "And your limp is hardly noticeable."

"Why you all worried then?"

"The baby could have so many things wrong, it would never be able to leave home and might need machines to stay alive."

"That sucks."

Yes, it did.

"I have to go, sweetie." Lilly patted Miranda's shoulder. "Please don't tell anyone about the baby until I say you can. Okay?"

"My mother doesn't tell people about me, either."

"I can't believe that," Lilly said vehemently, although admittedly she didn't know Miranda's mother. Her sister always brought her to the center.

"Sometimes, when she thinks I'm not around, she says she only has one daughter."

"Oh, Miranda." Lilly could have cried.

The young woman screwed up her face into an angry scowl. "I bet if you had a kid like me, you'd be the same way."

Lilly pulled Miranda into a fierce hug. "If I had a daughter like you, I'd be so happy and so proud, I'd tell everybody I met about my beautiful girl and how much I loved her."

"Then why don't you tell people about the baby?"

"I will. Soon."

"Why not right now?"

Yes, why not? Didn't she believe what she'd told Miranda?

"Okay, let's do it. Together." Lilly drew back and took Miranda by the shoulders. "Thank you."

"For what?"

"Reminding me of something important I'd forgotten."

"What's that?"

"Unconditional love."

"I don't get it."

"Don't worry." She pushed open the door. "I'll explain later."

"Wait, I gotta pee."

Lilly laughed as Miranda dashed into the bathroom stall. When she was done, they left the restroom together and went into the main activity room. Miranda bubbled with excitement. The others must have sensed something was up because all eyes were on them.

"I have an announcement," Lilly said when she reached the center of the room.

"Is Big Ben okay?" Jimmy Bob asked.

"Our mule is fine."

"Are we still going to the ranch tomorrow?"

"Shut up, you goon," Miranda scolded. "This isn't about you or that dumb mule."

"This is about me," Lilly said and waited for everyone to quiet down. "I'm very, *very* pleased to tell you that in five months or so, I'm going to have a baby."

Dead silence followed her announcement...for about three seconds. Then the entire room broke into applause and cheers. Those who could get up on their own rushed over to Lilly, hugging her, kissing her and offering her their best wishes. If any of them had suspected she was pregnant, they didn't say.

For the rest of the afternoon, she rejoiced with the center's staff and clients. No doubt her fears and worries would return the next morning. But she didn't let that stop her from treasuring every second of the afternoon and she could hardly wait to tell Jake.

"So, WE'RE OFFICIALLY out of the closet?"

"Yes."

Jake pressed the phone closer to his ear and smiled. Lilly had called to say she'd finally felt comfortable enough with her pregnancy to go public, and elation rang in her voice. It was nice to hear. With each passing week, Lilly and their child became more and more important to him.

"Well, good. I guess now I can do the same."

"You haven't told anyone?"

He absently stirred a pot of steaming vegetables on the stove. The girls were due any minute, and he hadn't seen much of them the last week. They'd stayed with him for ten days straight after Ellen's New Year's Eve wedding while she and her new husband went on their honeymoon. In exchange, he'd let her have his regular weekend. Reports from the family grapevine were that the reunion hadn't gone well. Apparently Briana and her mother remained at odds, and none of the girls had yet to warm up to their new stepfather.

Jake allowed himself a brief feel-good moment. He was

first in his daughters' hearts, and as long as he stayed there, he could tolerate another man living in his home.

"I did tell Carolina a couple months ago," he said to Lilly. "The day you went to the emergency room and had the ultrasound. She denies it, but I'm pretty sure she's told her mother. And if she did, you can bet my mom knows, too."

"What about the girls?" Lilly asked.

"I haven't said a word to them."

"Are you going to?"

"Yeah, soon. I may do it tonight. Ellen's dropping them off." Jake could only postpone the inevitable so long. Before he and Lilly could move forward, his children had to be told. Everything.

"Do you want me to be there?"

"Thanks." Lilly's offer and what it implied wasn't lost on him. "But I think I'd better tackle this alone. Depending on how they handle the news, maybe we all can get together one evening next week."

"I could make dinner. Or how about if I throw everything in a cooler and bring it over there?"

"I'd like that a lot." He imagined Lilly and his daughters sitting around his kitchen table, the all-American blended family, talking and laughing.

The vision promptly evaporated in a puff of smoke. Unless he and Lilly conquered the hurdles facing them and won his daughters over, those family dinners were going to be stilted and possibly angry.

"Do the girls like baked ravioli?"

"If it's cheese ravioli, yes."

"Great!"

Jake wished he felt as hopeful as Lilly sounded. He really did want that dream of everyone at dinner to become a reality. The girls were aware he and Lilly went out sometimes. Tonight he would tell them that he and Lilly were serious. Let them get used to the idea before he broke the news about the baby. With their home life at their mother's in such turmoil, he felt the need to proceed slowly.

He couldn't wait too much longer, however. Payson was a small town and tongues wagged.

"I hear a car outside," he told Lilly. "I'd better go."

"Call me later if you need to talk."

"What if I don't need to talk and just want to call?"

"That's okay, too," she said softly and hung up after saying goodbye.

He headed to the door, more optimistic than he'd been a few minutes ago. His progress with Lilly had been slow but was now moving in the right direction. It gave him confidence that everything would eventually work out for the best.

"Hi." He stood on his porch, waiting for the stampede.

His daughters tumbled out of Ellen's car, the candy-apple red convertible her husband had brought her as an engagement present. Jake wondered how long the shiny paint would last in the rough, mountainous terrain where they lived and how long until Ellen tired of driving a vehicle so ill-suited to a family with three active children.

LeAnne and Kayla nearly knocked him over. Before they could land in a heap on the porch floor, he swept them into his arms.

"I missed you so much. How are Grandpa and Grandma Pryor?" Over the weekend, Ellen had taken the girls and her new husband to Phoenix for a short visit with her parents.

"Good," Kayla chirped and extracted herself from beneath Jake's arm. Of the three girls, she was the only one who resembled Ellen, inheriting her mother's flashing blue eyes and thick brown hair.

"What's for dinner?" LeAnne demanded, pushing open

the door. She reminded Jake of his late sister and was a Tucker through and through.

He caught sight of LeAnne's hand. Her fingernails, normally chewed to the quick, were long, bright pink and covered with tiny decals.

"I'm glad to see you've stopped biting your nails." He couldn't say he liked her choice of polish, though.

"Oh." She held up her hand and wiggled her fingers. "These are fake."

"Fake nails? Aren't you a little young for those?"

"Mom bought them for me," she said, bounding into the kitchen.

Jake grumbled under his breath.

Briana was the last one inside and slow to join them at the table. When they started eating, she was mostly silent, answering only when asked a direct question and then limiting her replies to one or two short sentences.

"Anything wrong, honey?" Jake asked.

"Nothing."

He passed out the chocolate brownies he'd swiped from the dining hall earlier that day when Olivia wasn't looking.

His kitchen manager's last day was almost upon them. Finding her replacement had been a problem and had consumed much of his time recently. Then, yesterday, his other cousin, Corrine, Carolina's sister, called to tell him she'd decided not to re-up after eight years as a warrant officer in the army and was looking for a job. Next to Lilly's continued good health and lack of pregnancy problems, it was the best news he'd had all month.

"Briana's mad because Mom didn't let her drive her new whip over here," Kayla said with a sneer.

"Whip?" Jake asked.

"It means car."

"Huh." When did his bookish, somewhat nerdy daughter start using teen slang?

"Shut up, Kayla," Briana snapped.

"No fighting at the table," Jake warned both of them. "You know the rules."

Briana sulked. Kayla, unaffected, devoured her brownie. Jake said nothing more in an attempt to restore harmony; he wanted everyone in good spirits and receptive when he told them about Lilly.

After helping him clean the kitchen, the two younger girls vanished into the family room to watch TV. Jake didn't ask if they'd finished their homework—the rule was it had to be done before they came over. Because high school tended to be more demanding and Briana was often busy with extracurricular activities, she sometimes got stuck finishing up a reading assignment or report while at Jake's.

When she retreated into his office, he didn't ask any questions. Forty-five minutes later, he knocked on the door and entered, not surprised to find her on the Internet.

"Researching?"

"American history." Her tone conveyed just how little she liked the class.

He crossed the room to stand behind her, automatically scanning the Web page she had open. He was glad to see an article about the Industrial Revolution. Not that he didn't trust her, but in her current mood, he wouldn't have been surprised to catch her instant-messaging with a friend.

"I know you're upset about not being able to drive your mom's car, but try and understand. You've just got your learner's permit. The convertible has a standard transmission and a lot more power than you're capable of handling with your limited experience."

"I drive the tractor, and it's a standard."

"Your mom's convertible isn't anything like the tractor. Plus, it's dark outside, and the roads are still slick from the last snowstorm."

"How am I supposed to get experience if Mom doesn't teach me?"

While he hated seeing Briana's unhappy frown, he was inclined to agree with her mother on this issue. "I've got to pick up your sister's asthma prescription at the drugstore. What if we ran to Payson real quick, and I let you drive the Buick? The drugstore's right next to the ice cream place. I'll treat."

Her expression brightened. "I'd rather go to Java Creations."

"The coffee house?" Jake must have heard wrong. "You don't drink coffee."

"Dad," she said on a sigh. "Everyone from school goes there."

Briana drank coffee. Kayla used slang. LeAnne wore fake nails. His little girls were growing up so fast. Before long, less than two years to be exact, Briana would be leaving for college, finding a job—not necessarily on the ranch—meeting a guy and getting married. Kayla and LeAnne wouldn't be far behind. When that day came, he'd be alone.

No, not alone. He'd be with Lilly and their child.

A baby.

Diapers, late-night feedings, spitting up on his dress shirts. Then later, learning to ride a bike, the first day of school and another trip to Disneyland.

Jake was about to have a second family.

His knees buckled. "I need to sit down," he said and stumbled toward the easy chair.

"I thought we were going to Payson?"

"Oh, yeah. You'll have to drive. My stomach's queasy."

"That's the point, remember me driving?"

"Sorry."

"Jeez, Dad. What's with you?"

"Nothing. I'm fine."

He did feel a little steadier by the time all four of them piled into his old Buick. Then he remembered his plan to tell the kids about Lilly. The closer they got to the coffee shop, the more his agitation increased.

He considered postponing it, then was hit by a terrifying thought. Lilly had told the staff and clients at Horizon about the baby. Briana spent two or three afternoons a week with them at the ranch. It was possible—no, likely—that someone would mention Lilly's pregnancy to her. Briana was smart, she'd do the math and figure out he could be the father.

Difficult as it would be, he'd have to tell his daughters everything tonight.

Java Creations was packed, and the patrons, with the exception of Jake, Kayla and LeAnne, looked like they were regulars, Briana included. The two younger girls ordered hot chocolate. Briana got some decaf latte concoction with an extra shot of skim milk. Jake's request for a plain cup of black coffee was met with borderline disdain from the barista. He almost choked when she told him the total price, but kept his complaint to himself. If four overpriced beverages smoothed the way for his talk with the girls, he'd pay double that.

They grabbed a tiny table near the back, the only one available. It became abundantly clear to Jake the instant they sat down that a noisy, bustling coffee house was no place for a serious discussion, not with Briana hopping up every couple of minutes to greet friends.

"The best-laid plans," he muttered. No one heard him. "Let's go," he said when Briana returned from her third venture. Kayla and LeAnne were finished with their hot chocolate, and his stomach, uneasy to begin with, was rebelling against the coffee.

"Do we have to?" Briana glanced up from her cell phone. "It's only eight o'clock."

More like eight-twenty, and they had to be home by nine on school nights. Jake was running out of time.

"I have something to tell you. All of you," he added.

"What?" LeAnne perked up. Briana and Kayla eyed him suspiciously.

"Nothing bad." Jake's assurance made no difference. Briana and Kayla slunk out of the coffee shop. LeAnne skipped. "Wait just a minute," he said when Briana went to start the car.

She huffed and threw herself against the seat back.

He ignored her theatrics and mentally steeled himself for the task ahead. His daughters had been through so many upheavals in recent years. He couldn't possibly expect them to welcome another one, much less feel enthusiastic about it. Only the fear that Briana might learn about Lilly from someone else kept him going.

"You remember Lilly Russo?" He said the words he'd been practicing in his head during the drive there.

"She works at the center." Briana rolled her eyes. "Comes to the ranch all the time. The two of you dated for a while and still go out sometimes. But you're *just friends*." She mimicked him by drawing out the last two words.

"That's right."

"Are you dating her again?" Kayla asked, slouching in the corner of the back seat and fiddling with the hood ties on her jacket.

Jake reached over and patted her knee. Briana's constant bickering with her mother had taken center stage of late, and the other two were often, if unintentionally, ignored. He vowed to change that, starting right now.

"We are dating again. Sort of. And have been for a few months."

"Define *sort of*," Briana demanded.

"We're seeing a lot of each other."

"Are you getting married, too, Daddy?" LeAnne's innocent question triggered a shock wave that rippled through the car's occupants.

"No, I'm not getting married." *Not yet.*

"Okay. You're dating. Seeing *a lot* of each other," Briana emphasized in a clipped voice. "No big deal."

"Actually, there's more to it." He had their attention. It burned into him like three hot spears. But there was no going back. Not now. "Lilly's having a baby. She's due in July." He didn't add that she might not carry to term or that the baby could be born with birth defects.

One step—one bombshell—at a time.

"You're dating a pregnant woman?" Briana's expression changed, going from disbelief to confusion to outrage in a matter of seconds. Jake's prediction had come true; she'd done the math. "*You're* the father."

"Yes." Jake winced slightly. Falling off the pedestal was much harder than he'd imagined.

"Oh, my God! I don't believe it." Briana clasped the sides of her head with shaking hands. "First Mom cheats on you, then divorces you, then marries the guy she cheated on you with—"

"Briana!" Jake cut her off. He wasn't sure how much her younger sisters knew about their mother's previous relationship with their stepfather.

"You got that woman pregnant." She glared at him, her eyes ablaze with fury and—the thought of it turned his stomach to lead—disappointment.

"First of all, she's not 'that woman.' Lilly is a very nice person. You told me yourself you liked her."

"That was before I found out she was screw—"

"Enough." Jake clenched his teeth and took a moment to calm down. "We didn't plan on her getting pregnant. But regardless, I'm happy about it. Lilly's always wanted to have children and hasn't been able to…. This is her chance to be a mother."

"So, you're just a sperm donor?"

Where did Briana learn this stuff? School? TV? "No. I'm going to be an active, involved parent. Which is why Lilly and I are dating."

He looked into the backseat. LeAnne had crawled over to sit beside Kayla.

"It would be nice if you were active and involved sisters."

"I like babies," LeAnne said in a small voice. "Can I hold it and feed it?"

"You bet." He returned her tentative smile with a grin. Then he recalled how she'd acted with Jimmy Bob, and his grin dimmed.

Kayla remained silent and stone-faced, staring at the floor. Her reaction bothered him more than Briana's anger. His oldest daughter, at least, was venting her feelings, not locking them inside.

"Don't expect me to get within ten feet of the little rug rat," Briana spat.

So much for hoping she'd babysit. "Please don't raise your voice at me." Normally, he'd take a sterner tone with her but he cut her some slack tonight.

"Are you going to move in with Lilly?" LeAnne asked.

"No. I'm staying right where I am."

"Are Lilly and the baby moving in with you?"

"Maybe. Some day."

"Great!" Briana slammed her fist on the steering wheel. "I get to lose my room at your house, too."

"You're not going to lose your room."

"Right." She jammed the key in the ignition, and the Buick roared to life. "Mom said the same thing. But somehow I had to give up my bedroom and move in with *them*—" she jerked her head at her sisters "—so butthead Travis's butthead son could have his own room when he comes to visit us."

"Shut the car off, honey."

"I want to go home."

"Then let me drive. You're too upset."

"I'm not upset," she hollered. "And you promised I could drive."

"Briana, don't." Jake unbuckled his seat belt.

"Daddy!" LeAnne burst into tears and tried to climb into the front seat.

"Stay there." He gently pushed her down.

"Why does everything have to change?" Briana flipped the radio on full blast and shouted, "Why can't we go back to the way we were?"

"Shut the car off, and let's talk." He reached for the key.

Briana beat him to it and threw the car in Reverse. "I don't want a stepdad. I don't want a stepmom. And I sure as hell don't want a new baby brother or sister."

Lilly's worries about his daughters and their reaction to her and the baby were coming true.

Briana suddenly hit the gas. Tires spun, grappling for traction on the dirt parking lot.

Jake raised a hand to shield his eyes from the sudden glare of oncoming headlights. "Briana, watch out!"

He was too late. The car bucked and lurched to a stop as metal collided with metal.

Chapter Nine

"Are you all right?" Even though Lilly had spoken to Jake on the phone, been assured he and his daughters were unharmed, she choked up when she saw them in the emergency room waiting area.

He stood, and they went into each other's arms. "Thanks for coming," he said.

"I'm just glad you're out here and not in the operating room." She glanced down at his two youngest daughters huddled together in the chairs beside his. "Where's Briana?"

"She went to the gift shop to get us some bottled water. Kayla and LeAnne were thirsty."

"Was the other driver injured?" She reached up and lightly touched the small shaved spot and butterfly bandage on the side of Jake's head.

"No, fortunately. And the girls are all fine. I wouldn't have been hurt, either, if I hadn't unbuckled my seat belt. That rearview mirror packs a mean wallop." He grunted in disgust. "I didn't want to come here, but the police officer insisted when the damn cut kept bleeding. Then I couldn't get hold of anyone."

Though it was selfish of her, Lilly was glad his parents and cousin, Carolina, hadn't answered his calls. "Is your truck driveable?"

"We were in my old Buick, which is a tank, and it was only going a few miles an hour. The other car fared worse."

"Where'd you leave the Buick?"

"At the coffee house. The manager said we could park it there overnight. I phoned the repair shop, and they're sending a tow truck in the morning to pick it up."

"That's good."

"I know it's late and a huge imposition but can you take us to my place?"

"Of course."

"I've already called Ellen and told her the girls will be staying with me tonight." He looked down the hall and let out an impatient breath. "How long does it take to buy bottled water?"

"I can wait here with Kayla and LeAnne if you want to go search for Briana."

"Do you mind?"

In answer, she sat down in the chair he'd vacated. "Go on."

"I'll be right back," he told his daughters. "Stay here with Ms. Russo."

They nodded, the older one sullenly, the younger one more hesitant.

Lilly leaned in their direction the moment Jake started across the waiting room and gave the pair her most winning smile. "You don't have to call me Ms. Russo. My name's Lilly."

"I'm LeAnne."

"I know. I remember."

"Daddy says you're having a baby."

So, he'd told his daughters tonight. Did breaking the news have anything to do with Briana's fender bender at the coffee house? Lilly thought it might.

"I am."

"He says the baby will be my little brother or sister."

"That's true."

LeAnne's chatter was more curious than friendly but far better than her sister's silent hostility. Lilly swallowed her disappointment. She'd so wanted Jake's daughters to be happy about becoming part of her child's life.

If the baby was born normal.

Lilly wouldn't force them into a relationship with a child like her son, Evan. That would be traumatic, particularly for LeAnne, and too much to ask.

"I like babies," LeAnne said.

"I like babies, too. And kids." Lilly smiled, hoping for even a tiny response. No such luck.

LeAnne looked confused, and Kayla just plain ignored Lilly. She took the slights in stride. She had a lot of experience dealing with uncooperative clients determined to hate their circumstances. Given time, she was confident she could get along with, if not win over, Jake's youngest daughters.

Jake and Briana appeared at the end of the hallway. Lilly took one look at the teenager and knew her worries about Jake's other daughters paled in comparison to her fears about his oldest. Everything, from Briana's surly expression to her rigidly held arms, shouted anger and misery.

Lilly stood. "Guess we're ready to leave." She strived to maintain a pleasant and unconcerned tone. Inside, she was quaking.

She and the two younger girls walked toward Jake and Briana, meeting them near the exit. Lilly tried to make eye contact with Briana but the girl stared at the floor or the wall, anywhere except Lilly.

"Where's my water?" LeAnne asked.

"We didn't get it," Jake answered, his jaw hardly moving.

"But I'm thirsty."

"You'll have to wait."

Obviously, something had gone wrong at the gift shop.

"There's a convenience store up the road," Lilly said.

"Do we have to stop?" Briana whined. "I just want to go home."

Okay, thought Lilly. Not the right time to try impressing his daughters with helpful suggestions.

Outside, Briana resumed her fixation with the ground in front of her feet. Jake took the younger girls' hands, and they crossed the parking lot. "Which way?" he asked Lilly.

"Over here."

They wove between parked cars in an awkward, silent conga line. A familiar tow-away zone triggered memories of the day six weeks ago when Jake had met her here and Dr. Paul had performed the ultrasound.

It suddenly struck Lilly how different tonight was from then and how different her feelings were for Jake. Little by little during the past weeks they'd grown closer and she'd started falling for him.

Or was that falling for him *again?*

"I'm hungry," LeAnne complained as they neared Lilly's car.

She removed her keys from her purse and pressed the button to unlock the doors. "I have some crackers in the glove compartment." She reached for the driver's side door.

Briana, one step ahead of everyone else, already had her door open.

"That's all right," Jake said. "She can wait to eat until we get home."

"I don't mind sharing." Lilly winked at LeAnne as she opened the door.

"He said she can wait!" Briana wheeled on Lilly. "Quit trying so hard to be the nice girlfriend so we'll like you and be okay with you having our dad's kid."

"I'm...sorry I didn't—"

"Briana!" Jake exploded. "That was rude and uncalled for."

A strange and unexpected sensation bloomed in Lilly's middle. She placed one hand on the car roof to steady herself. Her other hand went to cradle her belly. She was vaguely aware of Jake barreling around the car.

"Lilly! Are you all right?"

She tried to nod but didn't quite manage as tears filled her eyes and blurred her vision.

"Is it cramps?" Jake took her arm and held her firmly, supporting her.

She leaned on him, waiting for the sensation to recede and—please, oh, please, God—return.

"No. Not cramps." She couldn't stop crying. "I just felt the baby move for the first time."

"You did?" Jake's grin stretched from ear to ear and his grip on her arm tightened. He kissed her temple and covered her hand with his. "That's great, sweetheart."

"Yeah, great," Briana grumbled. Then she turned around and stormed off.

BRIANA WAS conspicuously absent during Lilly's next visit to the ranch. Lilly, Georgina, Austin—a recently hired caregiver—and a van full of clients had arrived nearly an hour ago, and the teenager had yet to make an appearance. Lilly didn't think she would. Not after the other night when she'd stomped off, leaving Jake to chase after her and bring her back.

The drive from the hospital to Jake's place had been long, tiring and strained. Lilly and the girls hadn't exchanged six words. To compensate, Jake talked enough for everyone until he'd grown weary or ran out of patience or both. The kids couldn't escape her car fast enough when she pulled into Jake's driveway. His goodbye to her had been brief, though warm. Lilly had fallen into bed minutes after getting home, only to be awakened a few hours later by another fluttering in her abdomen.

How could a single night be so wonderful and yet so awful?

Lilly had anticipated a chilly reaction from Jake's daughters, but it still cut to the quick. Not for herself—she could survive being the bane of the girls' existence, right up there with their stepfather—but the baby would be their little brother or sister. She'd expected more from Briana, given her caring attitude toward the people from Horizon.

Excited chattering roused her from her ruminations. A dozen or so guests milled near the gate to the corral, watching a trio of young ranch hands bring out and saddle the horses they'd soon be riding. Dressed in spanking-new cowboy hats and boots, their jeans bearing designer tags, the guests looked every inch the greenhorns they were. One of the ranch hands went around to each person, passing out bright yellow plastic ponchos in case the weather turned bad.

The sight of so many people took a little getting used to for Lilly. Bear Creek Ranch had closed down after New Year's Day and had reopened this week on Valentine's Day for the new season. She and the center's clients had gotten used to having the place pretty much to themselves for the past six weeks. Lilly hadn't minded in the least. The ranch in winter was breathtaking with its snow-capped trees, wreaths decorating every door and smoke billowing out of the lodge's redbrick chimney.

If not for the cold, she'd almost want winter back.

A young child wailed despite his mother's attempts to calm his fear of horses. Lilly knew she should go check on the group from Horizon and see how they were doing, but she had trouble motivating herself to do more than sit and observe the goings-on. Since reaching her fifth month recently, her pregnancy had wreaked havoc with her energy levels. In the mornings, she felt she could tackle ten things at once. But by the afternoon, she was completely exhausted and fighting fatigue.

The golf cart's distinctive chugging sounded from up the road. Lilly automatically checked to see if Jake was in it and jumped off the log bench where she'd been sitting as soon as she recognized him.

So much for fighting fatigue.

She immediately began fussing with her pullover sweater and slacks. She'd started wearing maternity clothes since announcing her pregnancy and, silly as it might be, she wanted him to see her in them. To her great disappointment, Jake hailed Gary Forrester instead, and the two of them disappeared into the stable office. Ranch business, Lilly thought glumly. Well, she'd just have to catch him on his way out.

Jimmy Bob emerged from the barn and meandered toward her, his demeanor pitiful. This was his first trip to the ranch in almost a month, and now Briana wasn't here. No wonder the poor guy was depressed.

"How's Mr. Deitrich doing?" Lilly asked. The older man's Alzheimer's hadn't gotten better since he had started coming to Bear Creek Ranch, but his family reported that he'd become a little more cooperative at home and they were happy with any improvement.

"Fine," Jimmy Bob answered distractedly. "Cleaning out the stalls."

"Good. What are you up to?"

"Looking for Mr. Forrester."

"He's in the office with Mr. Tucker. What do you need?"

"The keys to the tractor."

"Did Mr. Forrester say you could drive it?"

"That's why I need to find him."

Lilly was relieved to learn that Jimmy Bob was seeking permission. He'd become surprisingly skilled at driving the tractor, but she didn't want him thinking he could take it any old time.

"You should probably wait a few minutes until they're done."

"Okay." With a heavy sigh, he plopped onto the bench.

Lilly bit her tongue, more to suppress a chuckle than to stop herself from reminding him that was where *she'd* been sitting. Besides, it was a good excuse for her to go check on the clients and staff. Anything to take her mind off Jake.

"You stay right here," she instructed Jimmy Bob. "Don't move."

"I promise." He nodded enthusiastically.

"I'll be back in three minutes."

Jimmy Bob had proven himself to be reasonably responsible and, as a result, they'd gotten accustomed to giving him a little more freedom than the other clients.

She went first to the barn, intending to chat with Austin and see how he was doing with Mr. Deitrich. The older man had a tendency to slip away and wander off. One time, they'd found him in a stall brushing down a horse. Luckily, the old mare was quiet and not the high-strung gelding Gary Forrester used for endurance riding.

Loud footsteps echoed through the barn aisle. Lilly stopped and spun around. For a brief second she thought Jake might be hurrying to meet up with her. Instead, the child who'd been crying earlier tore into the barn, his mother and an older child in hot pursuit. They caught up with him at the first stall—where he'd mistakenly tried to hide—and carried him kicking and screaming back to the group of guests waiting to mount up.

Lilly tried not to be judgmental of parents and how they handled their children but in her opinion the heated swimming pool or a game of Ping-Pong might be a better afternoon activity for that family.

Mr. Deitrich was emptying a wheelbarrow of manure into the Dumpster and happily carrying on a conversation with someone only he could see. Lilly would rather he talk with

Austin, and went to find out why the rookie caregiver wasn't within visual distance of the older man.

A high-pitched scream brought Lilly to a halt. It was closely followed by a woman's angry shouts. A sense of dread came over Lilly and she changed direction, rushing back the way she'd come. Had something happened to one of the center's clients? Who was the last one riding Big Ben? If only she could remember.

It was immediately apparent when she emerged from the barn that the young child she'd seen earlier was the one screaming and his mother was the one yelling. In the next instant, a ranch hand hauled the boy off the horse he'd been sitting on and placed him in the woman's arms. Sobbing hysterically, the child clung to her, wrapping his legs around her waist. The outraged mother lit into the poor man, raising her voice even louder to be heard over her child's cries. To his credit, the ranch hand merely stood there and took it.

The other guests backed away slowly, as if the scene was too ugly and too embarrassing to be part of. Lilly decided they had the right idea and turned toward the barn.

She glanced back over her shoulder. The few remaining guests were meandering off. In their wake stood a lone young man, his head hung in shame.

"Oh, no!" Lilly's eyes darted to the bench, though she knew it would be empty, and her stomach dropped to her knees. This was her fault. She shouldn't have left to go find Mr. Deitrich.

Breaking into a run, she hollered, "Jimmy Bob!"

He raised a miserable face to her.

Short of breath and near frantic, she took him by the arm. "What happened, honey?"

"Is this your son?" The woman redirected her anger at Lilly.

"No, but he's in my care. I'm the administrator of the local adult day care center. Jimmy Bob is one of our clients."

"Well, you need to keep better track of them," she said with a sneer. "My boy was almost injured because of him. If that horse had reared…well, you can bet my attorney would be in contact with yours."

"Please." Lilly did her best to remain calm. Firing back at the woman wouldn't help the situation. "Tell me what Jimmy Bob did."

"Is there a problem?" Jake stepped from between two people who had stopped to gawk, Gary Forrester on his heels.

"Who are you?" the mother asked. Her son had stopped crying and began kicking his legs to get down. She frowned but held tight.

"One of the owners here. How can I help you?"

She seemed quite pleased to be talking with someone in authority. "This…person—" she indicated Jimmy Bob "—took my boy when my back was turned and put him on that horse. Any…*idiot* could see he's scared to death and didn't want to ride."

Lilly disliked the woman's use of the word *idiot*. This, however, wasn't the right moment to educate her on name-calling or labeling special-needs individuals.

Jimmy Bob began to stammer. "I d-didn't m-mean nothing, Ms. Russo. I just w-wanted to help. Like I help Samuel and Joey and Miranda ride B-Big Ben."

"It's okay, Jimmy Bob." Lilly patted his shoulder.

"Excuse me, but it's not okay." The mother finally let go of her son, who hit the ground and dashed off to join his brother. "People like him shouldn't be allowed near young children. They certainly shouldn't be allowed to wander around a guest resort *unsupervised*." Her laser-beam glare traveled from Lilly to Jake. "I can't believe that you, as one of the owners, would permit it."

"Please accept my apologies," Jake said cordially, every bit the businessman. "I'd like to invite you and your family to stay an additional night, compliments of the ranch."

"We're leaving tomorrow. I have to be back at work."

"Another time, then. The front desk will issue you a gift certificate good for a year."

"I expect a full refund for the ride, since we're not going."

"Of course. If you'd like to take your sons fishing, I can have someone drive you to our private fishing hole."

"I suppose we could do that." Appeased, the woman called to her sons.

While she and Jake made the arrangements, Lilly escorted a distressed Jimmy Bob over to the bench. When he finally calmed down, she reminded him of the rules and his promise to stay put.

Austin appeared about the time she finished. "What happened?"

"Where have you been?"

"The bathroom. Joey had an accident."

"Where's Georgina?"

"With Mr. Deitrich now. She was with me. Joey threw a fit and wouldn't let me clean him up. Georgina had to help."

Obviously, they were becoming too comfortable at the ranch and too trusting of their clients.

Lilly also owed Jake an apology. The boy's mother might have been rude and insulting, but she'd also been right—the people from Horizon did need constant supervision and she had failed to provide it.

"Hey, Jimmy Bob."

She jumped at Jake's voice. What if he'd come to tell her their deal was no longer working and she had to find a new home for Big Ben?

"Are you okay?" He approached Jimmy Bob and clapped the young man's shoulder.

"I didn't mean to hurt that kid."

"You didn't hurt him. But from now on, let Little José help with any of the children, okay? That's his job, not yours." Jake reached into his pants pocket and pulled out a set of keys. He held them out to Jimmy Bob. "Can you hook the flatbed trailer to the tractor by yourself or do you need help?"

Jimmy Bob exploded into a huge grin. "I can do it."

"Gary will meet you behind the barn in ten minutes. There's a lot of hay to load."

"Thanks." He threw himself at Jake, hugging him fiercely.

Jake returned the hug. "See you later, pal."

Just when Lilly thought she knew the father of her child, he'd surprised her. "You didn't have to do that," she said, her mouth curving into a smile. "Jimmy Bob was left alone, and he shouldn't have been. Trust me, it won't happen again."

"The truth is that woman is nothing but a pain in the rear. The front office has received four complaints from her already."

"Still, Jimmy Bob shouldn't have taken her son and put him on that horse."

"No, he shouldn't have. But he meant well, and he only beat Little José to it. Both boys went riding with their father yesterday and loved it. The kid was pitching a fit for his mother's benefit."

Lilly stared at Jake in disbelief. "Then why did you give her a complimentary night?"

"I didn't like the way she talked about Jimmy Bob."

"Me neither, but that's no reason to reward her."

"It shut her up, didn't it?"

"Jake." Lilly's throat tightened. For what seemed like the hundredth time that day, she cursed her out-of-control hormones.

"Hey." He tugged her into his arms.

She knew better than to let him hold her in front of the ranch employees, and she sure as heck shouldn't let him do it with Georgina, Austin and the clients nearby. It violated every professional standard she held herself to. But Jake had defended Jimmy Bob and treated him like any other person.

More than that, Jake's arms felt good wrapped around her, as if they belonged there.

"What's this?" He set her aside with a lingering once-over. "New shirt?"

"Yes." She laughed and turned to give him a view of her silhouette.

"I like it. Shows off your baby bump."

"I like it, too."

"Are you free on Saturday night?"

"I could be."

"It's my aunt Millie's sixtieth birthday. We're having a private party for her in the dining hall after dinner. Will you come?"

She hesitated before accepting. This wasn't a simple dinner invitation. Jake was, in essence, bringing her home to meet his family. *All* of them. Including his daughters, who, as far as Lilly knew, were still unhappy about her and the baby.

He'd evidently read her mind. "We can't go on avoiding the girls."

"You're right. I just don't want a scene to put a damper on your aunt's party."

"Several of my tenants are going to be there. You're bound to have met some of them. You can use them for cover."

She laughed. "It does sound like fun."

"I'll pick you up at five-thirty."

"Okay."

He gave her a quick, almost platonic kiss on the lips. The tingle coursing through her, however, was a solid ten on the Richter scale.

"I hate to leave," he said. "I have an appointment back at the office."

"And I have to find Mr. Deitrich."

Jake had hardly disappeared before Lilly began having second thoughts about going to the party with him. Until now, her biggest concern had been his children. She hadn't worried much about the rest of his family, assuming they were like hers, loving and supportive.

But what if the Tuckers weren't? What if they felt just as strongly about her and the baby as the girls did? Could that be the reason Jake had said so little about his parents?

Now she wished she'd asked him before he left instead of letting herself become distracted by his kiss.

Chapter Ten

Lilly had met most of the Tucker family before, many of them at the Labor Day cookout just before she'd started dating Jake. But she hadn't been wearing maternity clothes then, and he hadn't introduced her as the mother of his child.

It did make a difference.

There were wall-to-wall Tuckers at Millie Sweetwater's birthday party, and the vast majority of them didn't know how to take Lilly. Reactions ranged from hostility to friendliness, uncertainty to curiosity, with Jake's daughters clearly at the negative end of the spectrum.

Jake's mother fell somewhere in the middle. She sat across from Lilly at one of the large tables, trying hard to include Lilly in the dinner conversation, showing an interest in the baby by asking questions—questions that most expectant mothers would be delighted to answer. Questions that indicated Jake's failure to mention Lilly's medical history.

"Have you picked out a color for the nursery?"

"Not yet." Lilly nibbled on her barbeque chicken.

"That's right. You don't know the baby's sex." Mrs. Tucker's glance took in Jake as well as Lilly. "Have you decided on any names?"

Lilly shook her head. "We're still tossing ideas around."

Mrs. Tucker's expression showed signs of strain. She'd gotten similar answers when she'd asked if Lilly had scheduled a maternity leave and enrolled in a labor class.

How could she explain that she was waiting to learn the baby's health?

"Are your parents coming out when the baby's born?"

"My mother is. She should be done with school by then." Lilly relaxed. Here was a safer subject.

"School? Is she a teacher?"

"No, she's studying to be one. She and my dad came out over Christmas during semester break."

"Yes, Jake mentioned that. You must miss them, living so far away."

"I do."

Jake reached for her hand under the table. "Unlike the Tuckers. We tend to live on top of each other."

"Which is just the way I want it, young man." Mrs. Tucker's scolding was filled with warmth and affection. She turned her attention back to Lilly. "I hope to meet your mother when she comes."

"I'm sure she'd like that, too."

"If you need anything, please call me."

"I will."

It was a promise she very much hoped to keep—because Mrs. Tucker, despite her obvious reservations, was the type of sweet, kindhearted woman Lilly wanted as a grandmother for her child. Especially because her own mother was so far away. Lately, she'd been missing her parents. Their visit at Christmas had been too brief for Lilly and she was thrilled her mother had agreed to return when the baby was born.

Jake remained by her side at dinner and for most of the party that followed. But eventually, duty called. His cousins had planned a *This Is Your Life* activity to celebrate their mother's birthday that required Jake's participation. For the last half hour, Lilly had sat in the audience, convinced that if she listened hard enough, she'd hear her name on everyone's lips.

If she thought this was bad, how would Jake's family react after the baby was born?

How would they act if the child had severe birth defects?

"Hello, Miss Russo." LeAnne bounded up to Lilly, her genuine smile standing out in a sea of polite, yet reserved ones. She laid a hand on Lilly's stomach. "Can I feel the baby move?"

"It's a little early for that."

"You said you felt the baby move." LeAnne frowned in confusion. "Why can't I?"

Her expression was so serious, Lilly had to laugh out loud. "What's wrong?"

"Nothing." Lilly moved LeAnne's hand higher on the small mound of her belly. "Try this."

LeAnne puckered her lips and concentrated.

Lilly abruptly stopped laughing. Would this child look like her or Jake? Would he or she have Kayla's button nose, LeAnne's dimples or Briana's stubborn streak?

"I felt something!" LeAnne beamed, showing two missing teeth on the bottom.

"You did?" Lilly thought it might have been her stomach gurgling and not the baby, but she played along, delighting in the moment and her budding relationship with Jake's youngest. Whatever could or would or had gone wrong tonight, she'd have this memory.

"I'm going to tell Daddy."

Before Lilly could stop her, LeAnne scampered off, and Lilly was left alone once more. But not for long.

"See, we Tuckers aren't all bad." Jake's cousin Carolina sat down in an empty chair beside Lilly.

"I never said you were," Lilly replied casually, as yet undecided about Carolina's motives.

"You have every reason to think badly of us," she said with mirth rather than rancor in her voice. "Especially if you judge the lot of us by Briana."

"She's a teenage girl."

"She's a lot like her mother. Very intolerant when everything in her world isn't perfectly to her liking. But have no fear. If you can give her time, she'll mellow, and one day you won't even remember what annoyed you about her."

"I can hardly wait."

Carolina grinned. "I bet you can't. And no matter what she claims, Briana loves babies. More than LeAnne. She could put herself through college on the money she's earned babysitting."

"No kidding!"

"There's one of her regular clients as we speak." Carolina pointed to a young couple with a baby Lilly guessed to be about a year old. "That's Natalie, our manager of guest services, and her husband, Aaron. He's another of the ranch owners."

"I've met Natalie in the office," Lilly said, "and spoken to her on the phone. I didn't realize she was married to one of the owners."

"Aaron is a Tucker purely by association. He was married to Jake's sister, Hailey. She left him her share of the ranch when she died."

"Oh." Lilly's mind raced. She knew Jake and his manager of guest services were friends. She assumed it was because they'd both grown up on the ranch. Not once during their acquaintance had Jake mentioned that Natalie's husband was his former brother-in-law.

"Yeah, *oh*," Carolina mimicked Lilly. "Things were pretty strange there for a while, very awkward if you catch my drift. We're over it now," she added airily, "and everyone gets along great. One big happy family." She nudged Lilly with her elbow. "It'll be that way for you, too. Don't worry. You just have to hang in there. Give us Tuckers a chance to work through our shock and jump off our high horses."

A commotion at the front of the room distracted Lilly before she could answer.

Carolina rose. "I have to go. They're bringing the cake out. If I'm not there to sing 'Happy Birthday,' Mom will disown me, and I do love being a member of this family." She held out her hand and when Lilly clasped it, said, "So will you."

Lilly joined in the singing, though her mind remained on her conversation with Jake's cousin. Afterward, while the cake was being served, she did attempt to see the people at the party through different eyes. It had been selfish of her to assume that only she, Jake and his daughters had been affected by their baby. Or that no one else cared.

She'd also been shortsighted, forgetting that even bad situations—like losing her first three children—could bring some good. Her marriage might have ended but she'd grown closer to her parents, discovered strengths in herself she didn't know she possessed, left an unfulfilling job for one she loved and met a man who supported her unconditionally where their unborn child was concerned.

Definitely some good.

She watched Jake eat cake and joke with his family, and her heart stirred with emotion. It wasn't due to hormones, not this time. Her feelings for him were real and growing stronger by the day. Soon she'd have to deal with them and try to figure out what the future held. But not here and not tonight.

As if he sensed she was thinking about him, he glanced up. His eyes, brimming with amusement a moment ago, turned dark and intense. Desire sparked inside Lilly. She hadn't felt anything this powerful and this consuming between them in a long time. Not since the night they'd made love in his hot tub.

Neither of them broke eye contact. Not even when Jake set his plate of half-eaten cake on the table and strode toward her. Lilly didn't remember standing but all at once she was on her feet.

"I'll get your coat," he said, escorting her from the room.

"Shouldn't you say goodbye to your family?"

"I'll call them tomorrow."

"I don't want to be inconsiderate." Or ruin the progress she'd made with LeAnne and Carolina.

Jake's cousin interrupted her conversation with an older couple to wave at Jake and Lilly on their way out the door. Lilly wasn't quite sure what to make of Carolina's knowing look and decided it was friendly.

Jake had driven his old Buick, so she didn't have to climb into the truck cab. Recently back from the repair shop, it looked as good as new. At the main highway, he turned left, toward Payson and her house. With each mile they drove, her pulse quickened.

What had altered between them so suddenly? And what would happen when they reached her door?

Lilly knew the answer long before they arrived at her house and had not one qualm about her decision. Jake wasn't merely the father of her child. She cared for him—far more than when they'd first dated. And he reciprocated her feelings more than when they'd first dated, as he'd repeatedly demonstrated in recent weeks.

"Would you like to come in?" She inserted the key in her front door.

"Are you absolutely sure?"

She heard his unspoken concerns and tried to put them to rest. "Very sure."

He cupped her cheek, then slid his fingers into her hair. She tipped her head back, giving herself over to the sensual tingling his touch evoked.

"I'm glad."

He lowered his head and skimmed the sensitive skin along her jawline with his lips, heightening her already soaring arousal. She'd completely forgotten about their surroundings. A passing car brought her to her senses.

"We should go inside."

Jake reached around her and opened the door. A rectangle of soft light fell on them from the entry-hall lamp Lilly always left on, illuminating them from the shoulders down. Jake's face remained in shadow, his expression hidden, his thoughts and feelings a mystery for her to discover during the night ahead.

Inside the house, Lilly removed her jacket. Jake took it from her and hung it along with his in the hall closet. She went into the kitchen, mostly because she was unexpectedly shy and uncertain of what to do next.

The sink felt like a safe place, so she went there, turning on the small overhead light. "Would you like something to drink? I have beer in the fridge."

"No. I'm fine." He came up behind her and rested his hands on her shoulders. He nuzzled the collar of her dress aside and pressed his lips to the hollow at the base of her neck. "It's okay if you've changed your mind."

She all but melted as his warm breath caressed her exposed skin. "I haven't changed my mind." Being with Jake before had been wonderful and exciting. Now that they knew each other on a deeper level, had spent countless hours in each other's company, she could only imagine how much better their lovemaking would be.

He lowered one hand to clasp her waist. His palm came to

rest on her rounded belly, and she involuntarily leaned against him, her back flush with his muscled chest. So much for leaping to conclusions. Jake wanted her with the same ferocity she did him.

"I can't wait to hold our baby," he said in her ear, his voice low and rough as he tenderly stroked the mound beneath which their child lay.

"Jake." If she could just be certain he'd feel the same after their baby was born.

In that moment, with his arms embracing her and his mouth tantalizing her, it was easy for her to believe he would.

"I want you to know I care about you," he said, turning her slowly to face him.

She could see the truth of his admission shining in his eyes, and it thrilled her to the core.

"I always have," he continued, his hands sliding to her hips and pulling her closer, his potent half-smile mesmerizing. "I can't tell you how glad I am you walked into my office that day with your proposition about the mule."

"Really?"

"That suit you were wearing was hot as hell."

She laughed. "I was trying to be professional."

"Business women are sexy." He seduced her with quick, light kisses. "You're sexy."

"I'm fat."

"You're having a baby. My baby. There isn't anything sexier than that."

He claimed her mouth in a fierce and possessive kiss that stole her senses. This was the Jake she remembered, the one who'd made exquisite and incredible love to her before their relationship had come to an abrupt halt.

His hands circled her waist, then moved up her sides. When he stopped just short of covering her breasts, she moaned in frustration. Winding her arms around his neck, she raised her hips to meet his, nestling his erection in the junction of her legs.

He stopped kissing her in order to draw a ragged breath. She thought he might take her into her bedroom. Instead, he stepped back and in one fluid motion, unsnapped his cowboy shirt and pulled it off. His undershirt followed. Both landed on the counter.

Lilly stared. She'd recalled every detail of his chest and torso, or so she'd believed. Their nights together weren't something she'd easily forget. Memory, however, paled when compared to reality. Jake was fit and strong and his muscles beckoned her fingertips, enticing them to trace the smooth contours. His skin, a healthy bronze even in late February, invited her lips to touch and taste.

She was helpless to resist, and she reached out to him.

He captured her hand in midair, and she murmured a protest.

"Not yet." He turned her hand over and kissed the inside of her palm, sending shivers dancing down her spine. "I want to see you first."

"Here? In the kitchen?"

"Kitchen, bedroom, anywhere you'd like. Just don't make me wait."

"The solarium?" Lilly asked.

Jake groaned his approval and swept her into his arms. He carried her down the hall and to the small room off the back of the house. The original owners had chosen to enclose the back porch with insulated glass and fill it with green plants that thrived all year long, even in the cold of winter. Lilly had added to the room by purchasing a double-wide chaise longue. She liked whiling away a lazy weekend afternoon, reading or napping in the bright sun.

At night, the solarium remained warm for hours. And if the

stars were out in abundance, like they were tonight, the view was spectacular—the perfect setting to rekindle a romance.

Jake set her on her feet, and she picked up the blanket she kept on the chaise longue, spreading it over the cushion. She felt his eyes on her, heard him unbuckle his belt. His jeans rustled as he pulled them off, and his boots thudded when they hit the tile floor.

She straightened and might have begun undressing herself if not for the touch of his fingers brushing aside her hair and tugging on the zipper of her dress. The fabric slowly parted, and she stepped out of her clothes.

Jake stroked her shoulders, her back, her upper arms. "You're so beautiful."

Any worries she'd had that he might not find her body as attractive as before her pregnancy disappeared when he turned her toward him. The solarium was dark, starlight and a half-hidden moon the only illumination. But Lilly didn't need to see Jake's eyes to sense the raw hunger burning in them. She could feel it—almost touch it—the sensation was so powerful.

She lowered herself onto the chaise, pulling him down beside her. He resisted, one knee propped on a corner.

"I didn't bring any protection."

She laughed. "I think it's a little late for that."

He remained sober. "I haven't been with anyone since our breakup. I haven't told you that before, but it's important to me that you know."

She met his intensely probing gaze. "You're the only man I've been with besides my ex-husband. The only one I've wanted to be with."

Jake came to her then, covering them both with the blanket. Beneath it, his hands roamed her body and together they discovered the changes resulting from her pregnancy.

He kissed her mouth, her neck, her collarbone and her breasts. His lips lingered on her stomach, his fingertips

brushing its gentle rise. Lilly sighed when his mouth continued downward, and his hands parted her legs. Jake had the
ability to make her feel utterly cherished, and tonight was no
exception. He brought her quickly to the edge but she stopped
him before she tumbled over.

"What's the matter?" he asked, his breath tickling her.

"Nothing." She tugged on his arms. In response, he positioned himself over her, his weight on his bent elbows.
"Everything's just right."

"I don't want to hurt the baby," he said.

"You won't," she assured him and inhaled sharply when
he entered her.

Their lovemaking had always been wonderful. But it was
more so now, sweeter and infinitely more satisfying because
of the months they'd spent getting to know each other and the
intimacy brought about by creating a child.

She climaxed, calling his name. His release came moments
later, and she held him through it, wrapping herself around
him. Afterward, they snuggled under the blanket, talking
softly and watching thin, wispy clouds drift past the stars.

"Are you sure we didn't hurt the baby?" He tenderly rubbed
her stomach with his hand.

"Dr. Paul told me weeks ago I could resume normal sexual
relations as long as I took it easy."

"Funny. I don't remember her saying that."

"It was during a phone call."

"And you didn't tell me?"

"At the time, I wasn't having any normal sexual relations
to resume."

"I'm glad we waited."

So was she. Too much, too soon was one of the reasons
their relationship had failed.

Jake's cell phone buzzed from beneath the chaise. "Sorry."

He kissed her on the lips before rolling over and fumbling in the dark. "That's strange," he said, checking the caller ID as he sat up.

"What?"

"Someone's calling me from my house." He put the phone to his ear. "This is Jake Tucker... Sweetie, what are you doing there?" he asked. "All right, calm down." Another pause. "No, I'm...with Lilly." He groaned under his breath. "Lower your voice, please." This time there was a considerably longer pause, then he said, "I'll be right there. Don't leave, you hear me?" He ended with "Call your mother and let her know where you are," and hung up.

"I'm almost afraid to ask," Lilly said when he was done.

Jake shoved the fingers of one hand into his hair. "Briana's at the house. She had another fight with her mother and drove there from the party. In the old maintenance truck, of all things."

"I didn't think she had her license."

"She doesn't. Only her learner's permit." He blew out a long breath as he stood, then began throwing on his clothes. "She went to the house, expecting me to be there." He sat back down to put on his socks and boots. "I'm not sure which one of us is angrier. Me at her for taking the truck and driving without a license, or her at me for not being at the house when she arrived."

Lilly wrapped herself in the blanket, collected her clothes from the floor and walked with Jake to the kitchen, where he retrieved his shirts. "Is she upset about us being together?"

"Not so much."

Lilly had heard Jake's end of the phone conversation and suspected he was minimizing his daughter's reaction.

"I hate leaving like this," he said at her front door after a last kiss.

"Briana needs you."

He stroked her cheek with the pad of his thumb. "There's

a lot I was going to say to you tonight. I feel bad about not getting to it."

Lilly did, too, but didn't add to his guilt by saying so. "You'd better hurry."

"I'll call you tomorrow," he said and left.

She closed the door after him, her emotions at odds. Jake was a family man; it was one of his most attractive qualities. Lilly couldn't be angry at him for going to his daughter when she was in trouble. And she couldn't be mad at Briana, who was having difficulty coping with the many unhappy changes in her young life.

And yet, she *was* angry. Or, at least, frustrated and confused. Everyone at the party had seen her and Jake leave together, including Briana. Had the girl's stunt been a deliberate attempt to sabotage Lilly and Jake's relationship?

She was afraid the answer was yes, and that Briana might never accept her and the baby.

"SHE WOULDN'T HAVE run away if you'd hadn't left with your girlfriend."

"Briana didn't run away. She went to my house."

Jake cursed his good cell phone reception. Usually, three miles outside Payson his phone quit working. But bad luck and an open passage in the mountains made it possible for Ellen to go on and on, blowing the incident with Briana out of all proportion. What else was new?

"She stole a vehicle."

"She took a ranch truck without permission and called me the minute she got to my house to let me know what she'd done and where she was." Not to mention hurl unkind accusations, which he'd chosen not to address in front of Lilly.

"Her behavior's out of control. We have to do something about it."

"You're right, Ellen. Maybe we should consider family counseling. For Briana and all of us. I could use some advice on how to deal with the girls." And how to bring harmony to their relationship with Lilly and their soon-to-be-born sibling, but he refrained from mentioning that to Ellen.

"Sure, blame them for your problems," Ellen said with disgust. "Briana's only giving us grief because you got that woman pregnant."

"Me? What about you? You're the one who—"

Fortunately, at that moment, Jake's phone died. He snapped it shut and tossed it on the passenger seat. What he needed to do—more than argue with his ex-wife—was think about what to say to Briana. Her actions might be sympathetic and understandable to a degree, but that didn't make her unauthorized use of a ranch vehicle, let alone what she'd said about Lilly, acceptable.

He pulled in to his driveway and parked beside the old truck. Angry as he was at his daughter, a small part of him took pride in her. He knew from personal experience that the truck drove like a tank. Briana had managed to make the three miles from the ranch to his house in the dark and on a narrow, winding mountain road. It seemed he'd been wrong, and she was capable of handling her mother's new convertible after all.

Briana sat curled on the couch in the family room, the TV on, but muted, and her iPod earphones in place. She yanked out the earphones and turned off the TV when she saw him.

"Before you start in on me, I admit I screwed up. I shouldn't have taken the truck without permission."

"Taking the truck without permission is the least of your mistakes. You broke the law. Your mother and I have good reason not to let you get your driver's license."

"Dad! You wouldn't." She shot upright. "That's not fair."

"I didn't say we'd do it." He sat on the opposite side of the couch. "Only that we have good reason. But rest assured, there will be a punishment."

"I figured as much." She sat back down, hugging the corner cushion.

"Why'd you do it, Briana?"

"I told you, Mom and I had another fight."

"That's not what she said."

"Whatever."

"Briana."

His needling succeeded in unleashing her anger. "Why'd you have to leave early—with *her?*"

"I brought Lilly to the party. Of course I took her home."

"And stayed there."

Yes, he'd done that, and it had been worth it.

"Lilly and I are involved. We're having a baby together."

"You don't have to remind me."

Okay…it was obvious reasoning with her wasn't going to work. "If you'd told me—"

"I couldn't. You left." Briana's face crumpled, her anger apparently spent.

Jake realized in that moment he'd been missing something important. "Why did you come here, sweetie? What's really bothering you?"

She wiped her nose with her shirtsleeve and said in a tiny voice, "I wanted to talk about moving in with you. Permanently."

"I see."

"You could act happier."

"It's not that. You know how much I'd love to have you live here. But your mother and I have an agreement."

"She has no say. I was talking to some other kids at school, and I'm old enough by law to decide for myself which parent I want to live with."

Who needed an attorney when they had informed friends? He tried a different approach.

"You'd be moving away from your sisters."

"Not really. I'd see them every day at the ranch. And Wednesday nights and every other weekend."

"Is that enough?"

"It is for you."

Ouch! "Let's talk about this some more tomorrow. I'm not opposed to the idea," he said before she could interrupt him, "but there's a lot to consider."

Like Lilly and the baby moving in. Many of Briana's problems with her mother stemmed from her feelings of being displaced, physically and emotionally, by her stepfather and periodically visiting stepbrother. The same thing could happen here with a new stepmother and baby, especially one who might need a lot of attention. "I want you to be sure you'd be moving in for the right reasons, not because you had a fight with your mom and you're mad at her."

"Yeah, I get it." Some of her defiance returned. "Everything's changed now that you knocked up Ms. Russo."

"Briana!" It took every ounce of his willpower not to respond in anger.

"Oh, please. What about all those talks you gave me on being responsible and abstinence and waiting until you're ready. Weren't *you* listening?"

He cringed inwardly. Was talking about sex with your children ever easy? Jake weighed his words before speaking them. He couldn't mess this up.

"Lilly and I didn't have indiscriminate sex. We care a lot about each other. We were also responsible and used protection. Unfortunately, it failed. Or not unfortunately, depending on how you look at it."

"What do you mean?" she said snippily.

He'd been planning to wait until next weekend to tell the girls about Lilly's medical history. Now might be better.

"Lilly's been pregnant before. Three times."

"She has kids?"

"No. Two of the babies were stillborn. The last one had severe birth defects and didn't live long."

"Oh." Not unexpectedly, his news appeared to disturb Briana.

"Lilly has a genetic disorder. I don't understand much except that she's always wanted children and hasn't been able to have them. Her doctor thinks her chances are better with this baby because he or she has a different father. And I care about Lilly and I want her to have a healthy baby."

"What if the baby's not healthy?"

"Then we'll cross that bridge when we come to it."

"You'd be stuck. You'd have to pay for that kid."

"I've never thought of myself as being 'stuck' with any of my children."

"Because it's your duty."

"A duty I've always enjoyed. I love you girls."

Just when he assumed he was getting somewhere with Briana, she showed him how very far he still had to go.

"Well, *your* duty shouldn't have to be *my* duty," she said and sprang up from the couch, snatching her iPod. "You're trying to make yourself sound all noble and everything, giving Lilly the kid she's always wanted. But the truth is you got her pregnant, and now we're all forced to put up with that baby in our lives whether we like it or not. A baby who could be born screwed up or even die. How fair is that?"

She fled the family room and ran down the hall. A few seconds later, Jake heard her bedroom door slam.

Some time passed before he moved from the couch. Briana might have thrown a childish fit but he couldn't dismiss her feelings or the painful points she'd raised. He wanted to be a good father to Lilly's baby. But in so doing, was he being a lousy father to his daughters?

Chapter Eleven

Lilly studied her computer screen, scrolling through the photographs one by one. Her mother had taken the pictures at the enlistment party of their neighbor's son, Peter, and e-mailed them to Lilly together with a long, newsy letter. The last photo showed him in uniform with his wife and their young baby, Peter's military cap perched crookedly on the child's little head. They all looked so happy and so...complete.

For several seconds, Lilly envied them. Fortunately, the emotion didn't last. She had much to be grateful for, including a job she loved that gave her tremendous satisfaction. If she never attained that complete family, she'd still have a wonderful life.

But, oh, it would be nice to have at least one child....

She imagined pictures of her holding a baby, Jake by her side. Would he be her husband or simply the father of her child? He hadn't proposed to her again, but as the weeks passed with more good reports from Dr. Paul, Lilly expected him to pop the question again any day.

She only wished she knew how she'd answer him if—and when—he did ask.

Lilly dashed off a quick e-mail to her mother. She thanked her for the pictures, told her about Jake's aunt's birthday party last week, and assured her of how well her pregnancy—nearly six months and counting—was progressing. She also officially accepted her mother's offer to fly out when the baby was born, saying they'd firm up a date later. Lilly's mother wouldn't be satisfied with that response, but she'd have to live with it. At this point Lilly refused to make any more plans than the bare minimum because of the risk that they'd change or become unnecessary.

She was both elated and scared to be approaching her third trimester. It was around this time that she'd lost her first baby, and she couldn't help recalling that terrible day. Sadly, those memories were sabotaging her happiness—and her relationship with Jake, which also seemed to be going well.

Clicking the send button, she exited her e-mail program and shut down the computer. Jake was due any second. They were going to the Payson Rodeo, an annual event that drew thousands of people to the small town and had filled the ranch's guest cabins to capacity.

What made this outing special was that they were having lunch with his cousin, Carolina, and her boyfriend, then meeting Jake's family at the rodeo where they'd all sit together. Briana, along with other students from her school, was performing in the opening ceremony.

Jake arrived on time, as usual, and walked Lilly to his Buick.

"I thought we'd be driving in your truck," she said, taking his hand.

"Carolina and Denny decided to come with us rather than meet at the restaurant. Then they'll hitch a ride home with my folks after the rodeo."

It was then that Lilly noticed the couple in the backseat. "Great." She liked Jake's cousin. Though they weren't quite friends yet, they'd been getting along well since the night of Millie's birthday party. "I finally get to meet the boyfriend."

"One of them." Jake shot her an amused look. "I think she has two on the string these days."

Lilly had gotten an earful about Carolina's dating habits. From Carolina, not Jake. His cousin made no secret of the fact that she had zero intention of settling down, or at least not for years.

The trip to the restaurant went quickly. Lilly took an instant liking to Denny, Carolina's guy *du jour,* and the four of them savored a lovely meal in the outdoor dining area of the restaurant. But Lilly's nerves kicked into high gear the moment the rodeo parking lot came into sight. She had yet to make the kind of progress with the rest of Jake's family as she had with Carolina and LeAnne.

His two youngest daughters sat in the bleachers beside their grandparents. Next to them were the Forresters, Gary, his wife, their daughter, Natalie, and their granddaughter, a squirmy and very pretty toddler.

Natalie's husband, a former national rodeo champion, wasn't with them. He'd retired from the circuit after his first wife, Jake's sister, Hailey, had died, and he now worked for a radio broadcasting company. Jake and Lilly had stopped by the station's booth on the way to their seats to say hello to him.

Jake helped Lilly up the aluminum steps to their seats in the bleachers. The girls scrambled over to him as soon as he sat down, chatting excitedly about their day and what he'd missed so far—namely the petting zoo, cotton candy and a trip to the icky portable toilets. Everyone moved and shifted to accommodate the change in seating arrangements.

For the second time that day, Lilly experienced a stab of envy. It was much harder to rationalize the emotion away when happy families surrounded her. Jake's daughters hung all over him, their small hands resting on his shoulders and knees. Even harder to deal with was Natalie's toddler, who giggled and squealed and reached her chubby arms out to her grandparents in a bid for attention.

Lilly might have gone on feeling sorry for herself if not for LeAnne.

"Hi," she said, squeezing in beside Lilly, displacing her father in the process.

"Hi, there."

Without asking, she put her hand on Lilly's stomach. "How's the baby today?"

"Good. Sleeping now, I think. He or she hasn't moved much since lunch."

LeAnne lowered her head until her mouth was inches from Lilly's protruding stomach. "Hello, baby." She gently patted Lilly. "Can you hear me? I'm saving all my old toys so I can give them to you when you get older."

Lilly lifted her hand, hesitated, then tentatively touched LeAnne's hair. The little girl had included Lilly in her family circle, and she was enormously moved.

She glanced up to find Jake staring at her, his expression tender and paternal. "What if the baby's a boy?" He addressed LeAnne but grinned at Lilly. "He might not want to play with your Barbie dolls."

"I'm not giving him my Barbie dolls." LeAnne abruptly sat up. "He can have Ken. I don't like Ken all that much anyway, not since the dog chewed his arm."

Lilly's laughter vanquished the last of her envy. However things turned out with Jake and the baby, she had a new friend in LeAnne and another reason to be grateful.

If only forging relationships with the rest of Jake's family were as easy. His parents' greeting to her bordered on reserved, and Kayla kept her distance, always making sure either Jake or LeAnne was between her and Lilly.

A loud electronic screech pierced the air, causing one of

two nearby people to raise their voices in protest. The arena
speakers crackled to life, and a male voice came on, announcing the start of the rodeo, which would run through Sunday.
Sponsors were acknowledged and thanked, concession stand
and restroom locations identified and a brief summary of
events listed. The emcee finished with a rousing welcome to
fans and participants alike and with that, the opening ceremony began.

A gate at the far end of the arena opened. Arizona's
reigning rodeo queen galloped out on a stunning palomino
horse, a flag of the United States held high. Everyone stood.
As she circled the arena, the national anthem played. When
it was over, the audience cheered and took their seats. More
riders followed, some dressed in period and Native-American
costumes, some carrying banners.

"Look!" Jake's mom shouted. "There she is."

Briana burst from the gate with six other riders. Bright tur-
quoise sashes identified them as the high school's equestrian drill
team. They trotted in unison to the middle of the arena, where
they performed a series of complicated dressage maneuvers.

Lilly was impressed. She'd seen Briana ride at the ranch
and practice her barrel racing, but nothing like this.

Jake's mother leaned into his father, and they shared smiles
that were both proud and sad. "She looks just like Hailey did
at her age."

"Like you did, too." Mr. Tucker patted his wife's leg.

Watching Jake's parents, Lilly felt a small connection with
them that she hadn't before. They'd lost a child, and that re-
alization gave her pause. Could his parents' reaction to her be
based on the fact that they didn't want their son to experience
the same type of tragedy they had?

The drill team executed their last moves and lined up in the
center of the arena. On cue, all seven horses went down on

one knee in an elegant bow. The audience applauded wildly, showing their support for the hometown girls.

Lilly jumped to her feet, clapping and calling Briana's name. She didn't realize what she was doing until Jake joined her, and so did the rest of his family. Lilly sat back down only when the drill team had exited. Jake put an arm around her and drew her close. They exchanged a lingering glance before he let her go.

The crowd finally quieted, and the first event was announced.

Lilly didn't see the saddle bronc rider explode out of the chute. Kayla stood in her way. She'd crawled over her father to get to Lilly.

"Were you really happy for my sister, or were you faking it in order to impress my dad?"

"Kayla," Jake said sharply.

"That's all right. I'll answer the question." Lilly looked Kayla straight in the eyes. "Your sister Briana and I don't always get along. Neither do you and I. That doesn't mean I don't appreciate her hard work and her talent, whether it's with her school drill team or at the ranch. I cheered for your sister because I was genuinely impressed with her performance. And I would've done exactly the same thing even if I was sitting alone on the other side of the arena, and your dad didn't know I was here."

"Okay," Kayla said after a moment and sat down.

On the other side of Lilly. Not next to her father.

Again, everyone shifted in their seats.

No one, Jake especially, seemed to mind.

"Good morning."

"Morning to you, too." Lilly snuggled closer to Jake, her cheek against his chest, her hand draped over his middle. Sunlight seeped through the partially open blinds, casting horizontal lines across the foot of the bed.

"Go back to sleep," he said, tracing the outline of her ear with a fingertip. "Just because I need to get up early doesn't mean you do."

"I wish you didn't have to go to work today."

"Me, too. But we have a lot to do to get ready for the annual breakfast ride. It's only six weeks away."

"Natalie said last year Aaron put the whole thing together in three weeks."

"It's bigger this year. And he wasn't a newlywed then."

Lilly almost hadn't expressed her wish that Jake stay home out loud, afraid he might misunderstand and assume she was ready to take another leap in their relationship. She was glad to see he'd treated her remark for what it was, a longing to extend the nice time they'd had, starting with lunch and the rodeo and ending with making love in his bed.

They hadn't been intimate since the night at her place, when Jake had left in a hurry because Briana had "borrowed" one of the ranch trucks. Thankfully, there'd been no interruptions last night. When Jake suggested Lilly come home with him after the rodeo, she'd agreed without reservation. Briana had been occupied with her equestrian drill team and wasn't likely to pull a repeat stunt. The younger girls went home with their grandparents. No one was quite sure where Carolina and Denny had disappeared to—nor was anyone concerned.

Jake hadn't told Lilly until later that he needed to wake up early for work. As much as she would've liked to sleep in for another hour or two, tucked securely in the crook of his arm, she understood. The annual breakfast ride raised a considerable amount of money for the Hailey Reyes Foundation, a nonprofit organization founded by Aaron and named in honor of Jake's late sister. The foundation and the projects it funded were near and dear to his heart.

"I'll call you a little before lunch." He kneaded the small

of her back. His strong fingers managed to find the very muscles that ached from sitting for hours in the bleachers. "I should be done by then and I'll swing by to pick you up and take you home. Unless—" his voice roughened and his hand moved lower "—you're willing to stay here another night."

"I don't have a toothbrush," she said around a yawn.

"Borrow mine."

"Or clothes."

"I have a pair of old gym shorts you can wear and plenty of sweatshirts."

"What about underwear?"

"Go without," he murmured seductively.

His palm slid up to her hip, and he pulled her against him, his breath coming faster. She anticipated finding him hard and ready and wasn't disappointed....

After his exquisite and thorough attention to her needs the previous night, she couldn't imagine being aroused again for at least a week. The desire winding through her and heightening her awareness was unexpected and thrilling. She embraced the sensations and returned the attention he'd paid her. When Jake finally entered her, after she'd driven him nearly crazy with her hands and mouth, she was already on the verge of climax.

She held out as long as possible. The instant they changed positions so that she straddled his waist, she lost every last shred of control. Seeing Jake caress her swollen breasts, run his thumbs across her nipples, sent her soaring.

Afterward, they lay in each other's arms, totally exhausted, completely satisfied and utterly content. Jake's idea of going back to sleep appealed to Lilly, and she closed her eyes. The lull lasted only a minute.

"Oh!"

"What's wrong?" Jake asked, immediately alert.

"Nothing." The glow within her blossomed and reached her lips. "The baby moved."

In the last month, the flutterings had given way to small jabs and jolts. Both her stillborn babies had hardly moved. She'd been too inexperienced during her first pregnancy to know that wasn't normal. During her second pregnancy, she prayed every day for even the tiniest twinge. There was none.

Evan had been different. He'd kicked and squirmed and wiggled and rolled. But then, his deformities weren't as severe as his brothers.

Lilly's smile faded as happiness turned into anxiety. If only she could be sure this child would be born normal, then she'd be able to enjoy her pregnancy just like any other expectant mother. No sooner did the idea of asking Dr. Paul about having another ultrasound enter her mind than she dismissed it. She'd been so happy these last few weeks and couldn't bring herself to spoil it by finding out the baby had problems.

"Let me feel." Jake put his hand on her abdomen. "Where was it?"

"Over here." She moved his hand higher and to the side. They waited for several seconds but nothing happened.

"I guess he's taking a nap," Jake said, his face glum.

Lilly didn't know whether to feel sad or relieved. He wanted so much to share her pregnancy and took pleasure in the simplest things. But becoming attached meant that Jake would be devastated if the child didn't survive or was born like Evan.

They hadn't known each other when Hailey died. Lilly had started working at Horizon six months after the accident. She'd heard how long and profoundly he'd grieved the loss of his sister from some of the staff members at the center and more recently, from Carolina.

Lilly didn't want Jake to endure that kind of loss again but knew of no way to protect him other than by distancing herself. He wouldn't stand for that, and she didn't want to stay away. Not after last night.

Her musings were disrupted by a sharp poke in her side.

"Hey! I felt something." Jake's face lit up. "Was that the baby?"

"Yes."

It was impossible not to take delight in his excitement. How wrong she'd been to think a devoted father and family man like him would ever be able to remain emotionally uninvolved with his unborn child.

And wasn't she the luckiest woman on earth to have him as the father?

He groaned. "There are days I wish the ranch would run itself." Planting a quick kiss on her lips, he hopped out of bed. "Stay right here."

"I really should get up." She threw back the blankets.

"Why?"

"To make coffee." Lilly didn't offer breakfast as Jake usually ate with his family in the dining hall at the ranch.

"That'd be nice."

While he showered, Lilly found those old gym shorts he'd mentioned and put them on, along with a tattered long-sleeved T-shirt he'd left hanging on a hook in the closet. In the kitchen, she found a canister of coffee and brewed a pot. When he came out to join her, dressed, shaved and ready for work, two steaming mugs were waiting on the table.

"Thanks," he said, sitting down.

"I figure I owed you after all the meals you've been feeding me lately. Lunch and dinner just yesterday."

"A hot dog and chips at the rodeo concession stand isn't what I call dinner."

"I had *three* hot dogs, if you remember." She attributed her enormous and embarrassing appetite to all the walking they'd done and the fresh air.

"You ate two. The baby ate one."

She started to make a snappy comeback about her weight but his sudden seriousness gave her pause. "What's wrong, Jake?"

"I like seeing you at my table, wearing my clothes."

"Oh." She sipped at her coffee, buying herself a few precious seconds to think. "Don't look too closely, I'm not at my best in the mornings."

"You're always beautiful."

She raised her mug. "Who needs sugar for coffee when Jake Tucker's around?"

He sat back in his chair, studying her critically. "You know how I feel. I want to get married before the baby's born."

"I do know, and I understand your reasons. But you have to understand my reasons for waiting to make any definite plans until later."

How long would it take her to get over Brad's ruthless abandonment and her fear of history repeating itself? Jake was a great guy. She was probably crazy not to at least consider marrying him. It was obvious he was trying and that her continued resistance hurt him.

"Okay. Forget the wedding. Move in with me."

"That sounds pretty definite."

"Not as definite."

"Your daughters may not agree, and if our relationship is going to succeed, we have to consider them."

"I also have a right to be happy."

"And what if the baby's stillborn or like Evan?" Lilly's throat burned. Their conversation was bringing back too many sad memories. "Do I move out after the funeral?"

"Not if you don't want to."

"There'd be no reason to stay."

"How do you know?" He pushed his plate aside and waited until she met his gaze. "Maybe there would be."

"We'd only be living together for the sake of the baby. If there is no baby…" She didn't finish.

"We have a lot of time yet."

God, she hoped so.

"Things change," he continued. One corner of his mouth turned up. "You could even fall in love with me."

Lilly didn't answer him for fear the unsteadiness in her voice would betray her. Not only could she fall in love with Jake, she was probably halfway there already.

AN HOUR AFTER Jake left for the ranch, Lilly began wishing they'd risen earlier so he could have taken her home. She'd cleaned the kitchen, checked the refrigerator and decided there were plenty of fixings for lunch—he said he'd be back by one at the latest—then tidied the bedroom, showered and dressed. Even after all that, three and a half long hours stretched before her.

Perusing the bookcase in the living room, she found a semi-interesting novel among the many testosterone-infused ones and curled up on the family-room couch, using a pile of throw pillows to support her back.

Her breakfast, for some reason, wasn't sitting well. Odd that oatmeal should bother her when the three concession-stand hot dogs the day before hadn't. Partway into the second chapter, what Lilly assumed was an upset stomach became mild twinges. Fearing cramps, she laid her head back on the cushion and tried to relax.

She must have dozed off because she was abruptly awakened by the sound of the front door opening. Was Jake home? She glanced at the digital clock on the entertainment center. How long had she been asleep? She climbed off the couch, a groan escaping her lips. Her legs and lower back were stiff from her awkward position on the couch, and her right hand tingled from lack of circulation.

"Jake?" She turned, her balance a little off, and massaged her stomach. The twinges hadn't lessened during her nap.

A figure appeared in the doorway.

It was hard to tell which of them was more startled, Lilly or Briana.

"What are you doing here?" Briana's eyebrows came together.

Lilly's first instinct was to defend herself. After all, she had every right to be there. But then, so did Briana. This was her father's house and, unlike Lilly, she didn't need an invitation.

"I'm waiting for your dad. He'll be here about one o'clock."

Lilly didn't elaborate but suspected from the further narrowing of Briana's gaze that she'd guessed Lilly had spent the night. Her father's gym shorts and T-shirt were probably a dead giveaway.

"Terrific," Briana grumbled and shot past Lilly, through the family room and toward the kitchen.

Lilly echoed the teenager's sentiments exactly. She bent to retrieve the book she'd been reading and rearrange the pillows on the couch when she was stabbed by a sharp pain in her lower back. Her first thought was the baby, but her concerns lessened when the pain began to recede. That would teach her to take naps curled in a tight ball. She wondered if Jake had any non-aspirin pain reliever in his bathroom cabinet—and how Briana would react if she saw Lilly going into her father's bedroom.

Briana reappeared from the kitchen, carrying a tall glass of orange juice. Ignoring Lilly, she plopped down on the opposite end of the couch from where Lilly had been sitting, grabbed the remote control and turned on the TV, adjusting the volume to one decibel below ear-splitting.

Lilly got the message and began to leave. Jake's back porch had a gorgeous view of the mountains. She'd read her book and wait there. A thought occurred to her and though it wasn't her place to ask, she did so anyway, her tone casual rather than accusatory.

"By the way, how'd you get here?"

"I didn't drive if that's what you're getting at," Briana snapped. "A friend dropped me off."

Well, that was good news. At least Briana and Jake wouldn't have another argument when he got home.

"I wondered if you'd be at the rodeo again today."

Briana's answer was to hunker down, her attention glued to the TV.

If she didn't want to talk, why didn't she just go to her bedroom? Lilly thought testily. It was almost as if Briana was staking a claim, challenging Lilly for position. Since Lilly was the one leaving, it appeared that Briana was the winner.

Lilly got only two steps away when Briana's head popped up over the back of the couch.

"Just because you're my dad's girlfriend, don't assume we're friends." She stared at Lilly, her eyes huge.

"I'm not assuming anything," Lilly answered calmly and would have continued to the porch if not for a sudden rush of moisture between her legs.

"There's something on your shorts." Briana's voice had a strange quality to it. So did her expression.

Lilly looked down and her legs nearly collapsed out from under her. Head swimming, she reached for the nearest handhold, which happened to be a coatrack. It teetered precariously.

"Are you okay?" Briana had stood and was coming around the couch.

Good thing, because Lilly was going to need help and fast. Jake's gym shorts were soaked in blood.

"Are so?" Brent had dried and was writing
briefed the...

...and finally pushed aside and came to grease...in and that
she didn't remember now fast he would work...

Chapter Twelve

Dear God! It was happening again.

Lilly felt as if her legs were refusing to obey her brain's signals and function correctly.

"Should I call my dad?" Briana's voice, thin and scared, came from far away and did nothing to reassure Lilly.

"No. Nine-one-one."

"Do you need help?"

"Just call."

Lilly stumbled to the couch, her hand clutching her belly. There was so much blood, she could feel it collecting between her legs, dripping down her thighs. If she sat down, she'd ruin the furniture's upholstery. But she really should be lying flat with her feet elevated. She remembered that much from the previous stillbirths.

Where had Briana gone?

Lilly battled a wave of acute dizziness. She had to remain calm. Stress made things worse.

She heard Briana then, speaking on the kitchen phone, giving the operator Jake's address. Lilly was grateful for the teenager's presence. She'd been alone when she lost her first baby and had called the paramedics herself. Her ex-husband had met her at the hospital but by the time he arrived, it was too late. The baby was stillborn. Because of all the tests she'd had, her second stillbirth had been expected—which hadn't made it any less painful. But neither tragedy compared to the sorrow she'd endured when Evan had died.

"They're going to be a while," Briana said. She stood in the doorway between the kitchen and living room, her cheeks a startling shade of white.

"How long's a while?"

"Half an hour. Maybe more. The lady said traffic is backed up all through town because of the rodeo."

Half an hour! It might be too late by then. The ranch was closer. Jake could be here in ten or fifteen minutes.

"I changed my mind. Call your father."

"I'll drive you to the hospital." Briana took a tentative step forward.

"What?"

"I'll drive you."

"How will we get there?"

"Dad keeps a spare set of keys to the Buick in his office." She swallowed nervously. "It'll be faster."

Briana was right. And what did the lack of a driver's license matter at a time like this?

"Get some old towels. Lots of them. Hurry," Lilly added when Briana was slow to react.

She waited on the porch while Briana backed the old Buick out of the garage and pulled it around. Lilly had shoved a towel in the loose gym shorts in an attempt to contain the bleeding. To her surprise, Briana left the car running and jumped out to help her down the steps and into the rear seat, where Lilly lay down atop more towels.

"Thank you," Lilly said, well aware that she was trusting the life of her unborn child and possibly even her own to the hands of a fifteen-and-a-half-year-old girl who didn't much like her.

About five minutes into the twenty-five-minute drive, Briana started ticking off the names of familiar landmarks they passed. "The highway department storage yard's coming up."

It helped Lilly to know where they were and how much longer it would be until they reached Payson Regional Medical Center. From her prone position in the backseat, she couldn't see much more than patches of blue sky and the tops of pine trees flickering past. The view was strangely pretty and very surreal, like a scene in a movie shot from an abstract camera angle.

"We're at Thompson Draw," Briana said.

Lilly focused on the baby, evaluating each sharp stab of pain, each clenching of her abdominal muscles. Was she having another episode of cramps or premature labor? When was the last time she'd felt the baby move? Had Dr. Paul been mistaken? Had resuming sexual relations harmed the baby?

"Little Green Valley."

The bleeding seemed to be slowing, or at least it felt slower to Lilly. She didn't dare move. Instead, she prayed. For the baby, for herself, for Jake and for Briana. Mostly for Briana, that she had the skill to get them safely to the hospital and not crash the car in the process.

"We're in Star Valley," she said, with less tension in her voice.

They were on the outskirts of Payson.

Thank God. The cramps—definitely not twinges—were strong and occurring more frequently. This was too much like her previous stillbirths, and Lilly began to fear the worst. Covering her face with her hands, she held back a sob.

One child, one precious baby. Was it too much to ask?

Briana slammed on the brakes hard, propelling Lilly forward. She threw out an arm, catching herself before she rolled off the seat.

"Sorry. A car cut in front of me."

There was that scared-little-girl voice again. Traffic was

bad because of the rodeo and the thousands of tourists in town. It was just as well Lilly couldn't see more than telephone poles, billboard signs and second-story windows.

"How are you doing, Briana?"

"Okay. What about you?"

"Hanging in there." Barely. Lilly was soaked in sweat, covered in blood and scared as hell. "I'll make it, don't worry."

She conveyed a calm she was far from feeling. Briana was having enough trouble driving as it was. She didn't need to know her passenger was close to falling apart.

"What's happening?" Lilly asked. They'd slowed to a crawl, and she wanted speed. Lots of it.

"We're in downtown Payson. It's packed." Briana hit the brakes again and uttered a swear word her father wouldn't want to hear. "Sorry. People are everywhere."

Maybe Lilly should have waited for the paramedics. Then, a wailing siren would have cleared the way for them.

"If you see a police officer, flag him down. He can escort us to the hospital."

They didn't see a police officer, but a mile and fifteen grueling minutes up the road, traffic grew considerably lighter. Not long after, Briana swung the Buick into the hospital parking lot. She drove straight to the emergency room entrance, flung open the car door and began yelling, "Help, help!" before her feet hit the ground.

Lilly rose up on one elbow and called, "Briana, wait."

But she was already halfway to the double glass doors. An unbearable pain forced Lilly onto her back again. A minute later, Briana returned with two nurses.

"Get a gurney," the first nurse said to the second after taking one look at Lilly. "Can you sit up, honey?"

"If you give me a hand."

The two nurses, one of them a man, were joined by additional medical staff. Lilly was lifted onto the gurney and pushed inside. They flew past the waiting room where she'd met Jake and the girls the night of Briana's fender bender and went straight to a treatment room.

"Wait out here," the male nurse told Briana.

Lilly hadn't realized until then that Briana had come along. "Call your dad for me," she said over her shoulder.

Briana nodded, her eyes wide, her lips set in a grim line.

After that, Lilly forgot about everything except saving her baby.

JAKE SAT IN THE chair by Lilly's bed and watched her toss and turn, fighting the effects of the medication she'd been given to help her rest. Even in sleep, her white-knuckled fists clutched the blanket and deep creases appeared on her normally smooth forehead.

The last three hours had been a nightmare for all of them. Her especially, of course. He'd seen the blood-soaked gym shorts before a nurse put them in a bag, and his stomach twisted into a terrible knot. It must have been many times worse for Lilly. And Briana.

He glanced over at her, sitting in a chair by the window, and smiled. His little girl impressed him. She'd gotten Lilly safely off the mountain and to the hospital. Quite a feat for someone who fainted at the sight of blood. There would be no punishment for driving without permission. If anything, he might sign the old Buick over to her on her sixteenth birthday.

"It's getting late. Why don't you call your mom for a ride home?"

She looked up from the magazine she was reading. "I'll wait for you."

All the rooms in the maternity ward were private and comfortable, providing ample room for family and friends.

"We might be here awhile. Possibly all night."

"No problem." She went back to flipping pages in the magazine.

"Okay." Jake didn't argue, he liked having her with him.

A few minutes later, Briana stood and stretched. "I'm going to the cafeteria. You want me to bring you back a sandwich?"

"No, thanks, sweetie. Not right now." His appetite had deserted him the moment she'd called to tell him about Lilly. He couldn't remember ever feeling so afraid and so helpless.

On second thought, he could. The day his sister died.

Not long after Briana left, Lilly stirred and moaned softly. Jake jerked forward in the chair and took her hand, rubbing the back of it with his thumb. Her eyes fluttered open, then went wide.

"The baby—"

"Is fine for now." He smiled reassuringly. "You're both fine."

"I only remember bits and pieces after the IV was inserted." She closed her eyes and sighed heavily. "I was in premature labor, wasn't I?"

"Yes, but the doctors stopped it." Thank goodness. At thirteen weeks early, there was practically no chance of their baby surviving and certainly not without serious problems. "Dr. Paul said she'd be by in a little while to talk to us. You're to sleep as much as possible and not get out of bed for any reason."

"I'm not going anywhere." She curved the hand with the IV needle protectively around her stomach.

"Are you hungry? I can page a nurse and have someone bring a tray."

"Not hungry. I am thirsty, though."

"Here." Jake poured Lilly a glass of ice water from the plastic pitcher on the nightstand beside her bed.

She took the glass and with his help, raised her head enough to drink from the straw. "Thanks." She grimaced.

"Are you okay?"

"Just a stitch in my side. It's gone now."

Something in her demeanor bothered him, and he couldn't quite put his finger on it. She seemed distant and distracted. It could be the medication. Or her exhaustion. More likely, worry. She'd almost lost the baby and probably would have if she'd waited for the paramedics to arrive or traffic had been worse.

"If you're hungry, go ahead and eat," she said, staring out the third-floor window at the late-afternoon sky. Distant mountains against a vivid blue backdrop did little to soften the bleak view of the hospital parking lot with its acres of asphalt and concrete pillars.

Maybe it was their mood that was so bleak.

"I'll wait for you. The nurse told me they could bring two trays."

"I'll be okay myself if you need a break or want to go home." Lilly didn't—or wouldn't—meet his gaze.

Jake had done much the same when Hailey died. But Lilly hadn't lost the baby, giving them reason, to Jake's way of thinking, to comfort each other, not retreat into themselves.

"Lilly." He waited for her to look at him. "Please," he added when she didn't.

Finally, she turned her head.

"You had a close call. But you're all right now. The doctors stopped your labor, and the baby's stable." He nodded at the monitor beside her bed, the one that displayed the baby's vital signs. "You have to keep believing that everything's going to work out."

"It was awful." Her voice cracked. "You weren't there."

"No, I wish I had been." He gripped her fingers fiercely. "But I'm here now, and I'm not leaving this hospital without you."

Her eyes brimmed with tears. "I just wish I knew for sure that the baby's healthy."

Jake handed her a tissue from the box on her nightstand. "He is. Dr. Paul did an ultrasound when you came in and said everything was fine."

She wiped her damp cheeks. "No, I mean normal."

"We could know for sure if you'd have those tests she recommended."

"And what if the tests come back with abnormalities?"

"Then we'll deal with it."

Admittedly Jake didn't always understand her. She knew he fully supported her decision not to terminate the pregnancy, regardless of any test results. So, why not have them and be better prepared for the outcome, whatever it might be?

It made perfect sense to him. But then he hadn't lost two sons and watched a third slowly die.

"Easy for you to say. You can't imagine what it's like to carry a baby that you know is probably not going to live long enough to be born or will die soon after."

No, he couldn't. Nor could he consider asking Lilly to go through it again.

"I see you're awake." Dr. Paul came into the room and stood at the foot of Lilly's bed to retrieve her chart. "How are you feeling?"

"All right," she said.

"Still cramping?"

"No, just sore."

Dr. Paul returned Lilly's chart to the bed rail. "Your labor's stopped for now," she said, studying the monitor screen. "And the baby's no longer in distress."

"For now?" Trust Lilly to key in on those words.

"First, let me reassure you that premature labor isn't necessarily connected with birth defects. Women with normal babies can go into premature labor. There are a dozen reasons for it. Our greatest concern is what we can do to prevent it from happening again."

She outlined her plan for the remainder of Lilly's stay in the hospital. At some point, they would take her off the intravenous drug used to impede her contractions and put her on an oral medication. Whether or not she went into labor again would determine further treatment.

"I'm venturing to say that when you're sent home, and I feel confident that you will be, you'll be on strict bed rest."

"How strict?" Lilly asked.

"You can get out of bed to use the bathroom, shower and dress."

Lilly gaped at Dr. Paul. "That's it?"

"That's it. Flat on your back as much as possible."

"For how long?"

"Depends on your progress. A week or two. The rest of your pregnancy if necessary."

"What about work?"

"They're going to have to get by without you for a while."

She glanced over at Jake. "I don't want to lose my job."

"You don't want to lose this baby, either," Dr. Paul said firmly. "And you will if you don't take it easy. You had a close call today, Lilly. Your body's giving you a warning, and you have to listen."

"Talk to your boss," Jake said. "He's been understanding so far."

"He has. But I wasn't asking for an indefinite leave of absence. The center can't run for long without an administrator, and he's too busy with the new one in Apache Junction to oversee both places."

"Let's worry about that later, after your premature labor's under control."

"You're right," Lilly said resolutely. "This baby's the most important thing. I'll figure something out. Maybe I'm eligible for temporary disability. I can call Social Security."

Jake didn't add that he'd see she had everything she needed and cover any costs her insurance didn't. They could discuss that another time, when they were alone and Lilly was feeling better.

Dr. Paul moved beside Lilly's bed. "Obviously, the longer you carry the baby, the better his or her chances of survival. Which is why you have to remain on strict bed rest. Gravity isn't your friend. Neither is stress."

"What if I go into labor again?"

"That will depend on how far along you are and if we can stop it with medication."

They discussed a few more details about Lilly's condition, the possibility of depression ensuing from the enforced inactivity and the extreme measures available if bed rest didn't do the trick. Jake hoped they proved unnecessary.

"I'm going to give you the name of a counselor," Dr. Paul went on. "You may find it helpful to talk to someone who's treated patients in your situation."

"What about tests for the baby?" Jake asked. "Are there any we can do?"

Lilly gasped softly. "Nothing invasive."

Dr. Paul considered. "Lilly's right. Amniocentesis and other, more conclusive tests come with risks. In her present unstable condition, those risks are even greater. To be on the safe side, we can do another ultrasound before she leaves the hospital."

After giving Lilly a brief examination, Dr. Paul said, "I have to leave. But I'll come back early tomorrow before office hours. Try and get some sleep. It's the best thing for you."

"Is there any reason Jake needs to stay?"

"Only if he wants to." Dr. Paul paused on her way to the

door and addressed Jake. "She's doing fine for the moment if you want to go home. The nurses will call if you're needed."

"I'd rather stay," Jake told Lilly once Dr. Paul had left. It wouldn't be the first time he'd crashed on a hospital waiting-room couch.

"What about Briana?"

"I'll take her home and come back afterward."

"You don't have to keep me company."

"I want to."

Lilly resumed staring out the window.

Jake once again had the feeling he was being ignored or dismissed, and he didn't like it.

"Mind telling me what's really wrong?"

"What are you talking about?"

"You're acting strange, Lilly."

She turned her cheek into the pillow. "It's been a difficult day. I nearly lost my baby. I'm entitled to act a little strange."

"I agree you've had an awful day, but I think there's more to it."

"I'm simply exhausted."

Jake wondered if he'd been reading more into Lilly's behavior than was there.

"Sorry," he said. "I get pushy sometimes. It's a bad habit of mine. I'll leave you alone so you can get some sleep." He'd travel no farther than the waiting-room couch he'd been thinking about earlier, but Lilly didn't need to know that. Later, if Briana changed her mind, he'd take her home and then come right back.

He stood, stretched and leaned over to give Lilly a kiss. She surprised him by opening her eyes. Then she lifted her head and clung to his shirt front.

"Forgive me," she said miserably, pulling him close.

"For what?"

"Acting prickly and out of sorts. I'm just so scared."

"I know, sweetheart. But don't be. Your labor's stopped. The baby's doing well."

"What if we go through all this, stop the labor and save the baby, and he's born with the same birth defects?"

"It won't happen."

"You don't know." Her voice was rough with emotion. "You can't know. No one can."

"I have faith. So should you."

"What if I lose you, too?"

"Impossible." It was on the tip of his tongue to tell her he loved her. Instead, he said, "You're stuck with me."

"That's what Brad said." Lilly let go of Jake's shirt and dropped back onto her pillow. "Only he divorced me."

THE DOOR CRACKED open, and Briana poked her head around the corner. "Can I come in?" she asked in a low voice.

Jake started to answer, then realized he should wait for Lilly.

"Yes, please," she said.

Briana stood by Jake's chair. "How are you doing?"

"Better than a few hours ago."

"Yeah." She chuckled nervously. "That was a pretty intense ride. I freaked when the van pulled in front of me."

"I want to thank you, Briana," Lilly said. "You saved my baby's life, and I can never repay you."

"Really. It's no big deal." Briana tried to appear unconcerned but Jake knew better. He'd seen her horror-stricken face when he'd arrived at the hospital. Comforted her as she shook from head to toe.

"It is a big deal," Lilly continued, "considering you have every reason to resent me and the baby. Somebody else— somebody with a less generous spirit—might have left me to fend for myself."

"I don't resent either of you," Briana said adamantly, then added in a whisper, "not anymore."

Never had Jake loved his oldest daughter more. No wonder Lilly fought so hard to have a child of her own. He wouldn't trade parenthood for anything.

"I'm very glad," she said, also in a whisper. For the first time since Jake had been at the hospital, a faint smile touched her lips. "I know it's a lot to ask, and if you say no, I'd understand completely." Her fingers plucked nervously at the sheet.

"What?" Briana asked.

"I'm not sure how long I'll be in the hospital. Another day or two, anyway. Maybe longer. Is there any chance you can help supervise the clients when they're at the ranch? If you're busy with school—"

"No problem. I'll help. I like doing it."

"Thanks. It's means a lot to me."

"It means a lot to me, too." Jake took his daughter's hand and kissed the back of it.

"Dad." Briana looked pained. "Don't go all mushy. It's embarrassing."

"It's unavoidable. Just wait until you're a parent." He coughed abruptly. "On second thought, let's hold off on that for another ten years, okay? You're not ready. *I'm* not ready."

His remark earned him a groan.

"I'm going to check out the gift shop," Briana said and held out her hand. "Can I have five dollars for another magazine?"

"I'll walk you to the door."

"Oh, Dad." She rolled her eyes.

Jake touched Lilly's hand. "I'll only be a minute."

"No hurry." Her eyes had drifted shut.

Good, he thought, she needed her rest.

Jake detained Briana just outside Lilly's hospital room. He

left the door partially open in case she called out or the monitors beeped, indicating the baby was in distress.

"I really appreciate what you did today and what you're going to do for Lilly." He pulled her to him. "You're a great kid."

"Maybe not so great." She withdrew from his hug.

"Why would you say that?"

"I'm still mad at you, Dad."

"What for?"

"You made me, Kayla and LeAnne start to like Lilly. And Leanne can't wait to be a big sister."

"Sorry, but I don't see anything wrong with that."

"Yeah? Well, what if Lilly loses the baby? Or it's born…sick like her other ones? The two of you aren't the only people who're going to be hurt and sad." Her voice caught, and she struggled for control.

Jake was momentarily stunned. He hadn't thought of that. He'd been too focused on getting the girls to accept Lilly and a new sibling.

"Grandma, too," Briana added. "She's crocheting baby blankets and stuff."

"We have to believe the baby's going to be fine."

"But what if it's not?" She sniffed and wiped her eyes with the back of her hand. "I don't want to lose a little brother or sister, too."

"Shh, don't cry." Jake kissed the top of her head because he really didn't know what to say. Maybe Lilly was right not to plan too far ahead. "I'll see you in a little bit."

Briana left once he'd handed over a five-dollar bill.

When he went back into Lilly's room, he noticed that her eyes were open. She quickly closed them and turned her head toward the window. Within seconds, her breathing slowed.

Jake sat in the chair, unsure if she'd heard any of his conversation with Briana. And if she had, what she'd made of it.

Chapter Thirteen

"Hey, Mom." Lilly stepped out of her bathroom, fresh from the shower, a towel around her hair. "You don't have to do that."

"I don't mind." Claire Russo was in the middle of changing the sheets on Lilly's bed.

"I'll help." She reached for a clean pillow case.

"You'll do no such thing, young lady. No lifting or exerting yourself. You heard the doctor."

"It's a *pillow*."

Claire pointed to an antique pine chest Lilly had purchased soon after moving to Payson and kept at the foot of her bed. "Sit."

Lilly complied. She'd been on strict bed rest since coming home the previous week after an eight-day stay at the hospital. In addition to showering, dressing and using the bathroom, she was allowed to eat at the kitchen table. That was all except for moving twice daily between the bed and the couch.

The disadvantages of being bedridden were numerous, inactivity being the worst. Her life revolved around the TV, the phone, e-mails and surfing new-mother Internet Web sites, in-bed exercises, Sudoku puzzles, napping and visitors. The novelty had worn off by day two.

She retrieved a comb from her bathrobe pocket and began working on the knots in her hair.

"Here, let me do that." Claire abandoned making the bed and took the comb from Lilly's hands.

Not for the first time since her mother had traveled from Albuquerque last week to stay with her, she felt like a little girl again. It wasn't all bad. True, her mother often got carried away, and the fussing and hovering irritated Lilly. But other times, like now, when her spirits were low and sinking lower by the minute, she enjoyed the pampering.

The anticontraction medication Dr. Paul had put Lilly on had some unpleasant side effects. So did the one that aided in developing her baby's lungs. The eight glasses of water a day she was required to drink made her wake several times during the night and stumble to the bathroom.

She didn't mind. Every imposition, every sacrifice, would be worth it in the end, or so she prayed.

Dr. Paul dropped by every Tuesday and Friday to examine Lilly. They'd vetoed in-home monitoring equipment. In Dr. Paul's opinion, it was costly and did nothing to prevent preterm labor. She'd expressed satisfaction with Lilly's progress and hinted at the possibility of upgrading her to modified bed rest in a few weeks. She would still have restrictions but nothing as difficult as lying on her back twenty-two hours a day.

Lilly missed going outside. She missed work more. The phone calls from her boss and staff—once frequent enough to be considered bothersome—had dwindled significantly. The thought that they were learning to cope without her contributed to Lilly's low spirits. As did her money concerns and the lack of a steady income. Though she'd gladly give up her job—and her paycheck—for a healthy child, she loved the center and loved feeling needed.

Groaning softly, she shifted her weight to her other hip, which only marginally relieved the chronic stiffness in her neck and back. Pillows and hot showers helped, as did the daily back rubs her mother gave her, but the pain never truly went away and always returned a short while later.

"Your dad called this morning." Claire braided Lilly's hair and tied it.

"Is he miserable without you?"

"He's managing. Your brother's checking in on him every day."

"How's *he* managing?" Lilly's father alternated between being the most annoying and the most terrific guy in the world. The same could be said about her brother.

"Okay. When they're not at each other's throats, they're getting along great."

"If I haven't told you lately, Mom, thanks for coming out."

Claire resumed making the bed. "It's been a while since your dad and I had separate vacations. I'm sort of enjoying it."

"Taking care of me is no vacation."

Lilly was well aware of how much trouble she was, most of it unintentional, some of it admittedly not. She was her father's daughter, after all. And strict bed rest wasn't fun. There were days, like today, when the tedium really got to her. Fortunately, her mother was well-practiced in the art of patience.

She wasn't the only one. Jake, who visited Lilly almost every day, ranked right up there with her mother.

"It's not as bad as you think," Claire said, turning down the comforter and plumping the pillows.

Lilly half sat, half lay in bed, her back against the headboard.

Without asking, Claire took a bottle of lotion from the nightstand and perched on the edge of the mattress. She placed one of Lilly's feet, swollen from water retention and from being unable to walk, in her lap and began rubbing lotion into it. Lilly almost cried, the massage felt so good.

"How long do you think you can stay?"

"Don't worry about that," Claire said, unconcerned.

"What about school? You've worked so hard." Her mother's lifelong dream was to teach, and she'd returned to college the previous year to obtain her teaching degree.

"I can take the classes again next semester."

Lilly hated being such an imposition but dreaded the day her mother would leave. Fussing and hovering aside, she'd come to depend on her and didn't know how she'd survive if her bed rest continued for three more months. Who else would see to her every need, fix her meals, entertain her, act as her personal secretary and rub her aching back and swollen feet?

Jake.

He'd do considerably more for her if she let him. Her mother's continued stay was a built-in excuse to keep him at arm's length and one Lilly frequently used.

She couldn't explain the change that had come over her since nearly losing the baby. From the moment she awoke in the hospital bed, reliving the terror of her previous stillbirths, she'd been reevaluating her and Jake's relationship. Hearing his conversation with Briana outside her door had strengthened her concerns and doubts and her commitment to wait until after the baby's birth before deciding how she and Jake should proceed.

Claire started on Lilly's other foot. "I told your dad when he called this morning that I'm here as long as you need me. He and school will both be there when I get back."

Though it was selfish of her, Lilly wanted that date to be well into the future. Every day she went without going into labor was a blessing. She'd been studying premature birth during her convalescence. Modern medicine had made great strides in recent years, but a child born twelve weeks early could suffer grave complications.

Lilly also visited Web sites dedicated to parents of preemies and read many stories that gave her hope and encouragement. If she could just hold on…

The phone on her nightstand rang. She reached over and picked it up, checking caller ID first.

"Hello, Jake."

Claire grinned at Lilly and left the bedroom. She could tell her mother approved of Jake and wouldn't mind having him as a son-in-law. She also liked his girls, who'd visited a few days ago. Neither Lilly nor her younger brother had children yet, and it was obvious her mother had been bitten by the grandchild bug.

"How you doing today?" Jake asked.

"Oh, fine." Lilly tried to sound chipper.

He wasn't fooled. "Something wrong?"

"I didn't sleep very well last night." It was the truth, but not why she was down in the dumps.

Dr. Paul had warned Lilly about possible mood swings and depression caused by isolation and inactivity. Lilly, to her displeasure, had become a statistic.

"Maybe I can cheer you up."

"How's that?"

"Lunch. I thought I'd stop by Ernesto's and pick up some Chicken Marsala."

No wonder her mother liked Jake so much; Chicken Marsala was one of her favorite dishes. Did Jake know or had he hit the mark by sheer luck?

Lilly's first instinct was to refuse his offer—that unexplained need to keep him at a distance rearing its head again. She didn't, however. Her mother deserved a nice lunch, one she didn't have to cook or clean up after.

"Thanks. That'd be great."

"Is eleven okay? It's a little early but I have to be back at the ranch by one."

"Sure." The ranch. Another place Lilly missed.

From all reports, the riding program was going well. Briana, true to her promise, helped the center's clients as much as possible. There'd been no more incidents since the one with Jimmy Bob and the little boy, thank goodness, and corrective shoeing continued to minimize Big Ben's lameness.

Of all the new ideas Lilly had introduced at Horizon, this was the best. She only regretted that she wasn't still an active part of it.

Soon, she told herself and tried to imagine her and Jake standing by the corral fence, their baby in a stroller. The image didn't quite come into focus.

"I have an appointment with some people you may know," Jake said, cutting into her thoughts.

"Who?"

"Jimmy Bob's parents." She could hear a smile in Jake's voice.

"Really! What for?"

"To discuss hiring him on part-time."

"Are you serious?"

"Sure. He's doing a good job. The hands like him, and he's a hard worker."

"Be honest. He's doing a mediocre job."

"What he lacks in ability he makes up for in enthusiasm. Besides, I'm not paying him much."

"Jimmy Bob must be thrilled."

Lilly was grateful and deeply touched. Part of the center's goal was to teach skills that special-needs individuals could use in the outside world. One of them actually landing a job, menial and low-paying though it might be, was cause for celebration.

"He doesn't know yet."

She wished she could be there. "What a nice surprise."

"I'll let you get off the phone," Jake said. "See you in a few hours."

"It's not like I have a lot to do." For someone who supposedly believed her feelings had changed, Lilly was reluctant
to hang up on Jake. Her world had shrunk so much recently,
and he was a link to what lay beyond it.

"You sure you're okay, sweetheart? You sound kind of down."

"Nothing some Chicken Marsala won't fix." She knew he
worried about her frame of mind.

"Everything all right with the baby?"

"Yup. Kicking up a storm this morning."

"Glad to hear it."

They said their goodbyes, and Lilly returned the phone to
its cradle. Thinking about Jimmy Bob brought a smile to her
lips and gave her the motivation she needed to get out of bed
and dress. In honor of the lunch Jake was bringing, she opted
for stretch slacks and a maternity smock rather than the sweat-
pants or lounging pajamas she usually wore.

She padded out to the couch where she'd lie until Jake
arrived. Her laptop sat on the coffee table, and next to it, the
TV remote. Changing her mind, Lilly went to the solarium
instead. TV and e-mail held no appeal for her this morning.

The chaise longue, bathed in warm morning sunlight,
released a flood of memories of the night she and Jake had
made love there. How different things had been then. She and
Jake were exploring their new relationship and optimistic
about the baby. Now she fretted endlessly about the baby's
health and whether she and Jake cared enough about each
other to make a go of it. He was certainly trying.

Thank goodness his daughters' feelings had changed—or
maybe not. Briana's conversation with Jake outside Lilly's
hospital door had given her more worries and further complicated the situation.

"There you are." Claire stopped just inside the solarium
and rested her hand on the door. "Need anything?"

"No. And don't fix lunch," Lilly added. "Jake's bringing it. Chicken Marsala."

"How nice." Claire's face lit up, probably as much at the prospect of seeing Jake as eating one of her favorite meals. "How long's he staying?"

"I'm not sure. Why?"

"I have to run to the post office, then drop off those DVDs we rented."

"I don't need a babysitter, Mom."

"It's not that. I figured you might like some private time with him." When Lilly didn't respond right away, Claire asked, "You two having problems?"

"You mean besides my high-risk pregnancy and the odds of our child being born with severe birth defects?"

"Jake seems like the sort of man who can handle it."

"Only because he doesn't know what he's in for."

"Don't underestimate him." Claire's tone softened. "He isn't like Brad, and you shouldn't lump him in the same category."

"He isn't like Brad. But then, Brad wasn't always such a jerk, either. He changed after Evan was born."

"That's true."

"I wish I could be sure that Jake wouldn't change, too, if the baby's born with a trisomy disorder."

"THANK YOU FOR lunch, Jake." Claire gathered their plates from the table and carried them to the kitchen sink. "It was delicious."

"Anytime." He'd grown fond of Lilly's mother in their short acquaintance and had the impression the feeling was mutual. "Let me help you with those."

"Nonsense. You stay put. I'm just going to throw these in the dishwasher and then get out of your hair."

Taking in Lilly's carefully averted gaze, he couldn't help

thinking there was a conspiracy at hand. But not one in which she willingly participated. He didn't mind Claire's less-than-subtle matchmaking attempts; he'd been wanting to get Lilly alone for over a week and had been carrying the small ring in his pocket every day, just in case.

Thanks to Claire, his wait was over.

"Couch or bed?" he asked Lilly.

She raised her head. "What about the solarium? I could do with a different setting."

He wished her smile was less forced and more genuine. Chronic bed rest was no fun, and he was becoming concerned about her. Each time he visited, she seemed more despondent, more troubled, more introverted. He had a plan, one he hoped would lift her spirits and give her something to look forward to.

If it didn't backfire. She'd turned him down once before.

"Solarium it is." He pulled her chair out and rested his hand lightly on her back as they left the kitchen.

Claire's parting goodbye smile was everything he wished Lilly's was. What would her mother say if she knew his intentions? His gut instinct told him she'd approve. Believing he had an ally boosted his confidence and convinced him he was doing the right thing.

The lush, earthy scent of green plants surrounded them the moment they stepped through the door. Sunlight streamed in through the skylights and glass windows, warming the rocks and stone walkway beneath their feet.

"I don't think I've ever been here during the day. It's beautiful."

Lilly sent him a look that said she remembered every detail about the night they'd made love here. It was an experience he wouldn't mind repeating during the day. Later. After the baby was born.

She gingerly eased herself onto the chaise. The only other

piece of furniture in the solarium was a patio chair at the other end. Jake considered bringing it over but then Lilly scooted sideways and said, "Sit here."

His heart beat faster. Everything was falling into place perfectly.

They didn't cuddle quite as cozily as they had before. Nonetheless, it was nice to sit beside her, and, after several minutes of small talk, Jake sensed her relaxing. The time continued to tick by and when the right opening didn't come, he began to get nervous. He'd have to leave soon in order to meet Jimmy Bob and his parents at the ranch.

Jake decided to make his own opening.

"What's the latest Dr. Paul says about you carrying to term?"

"She hasn't quoted percentages." Lilly made a face. "I think she's being intentionally vague."

"Why?"

"So I'll focus on the positive. Everything I've been reading says the possibility of going into preterm labor again is high. Stress increases the chances."

"I might have a solution," he said, smiling.

"What?" She seemed more wary than excited.

He reached in his pocket and pulled out the ring. The single sapphire, set inside a circle of tiny diamonds, glittered in the sunlight.

Lilly gasped softly. "Jake."

"It was my grandmother's. My grandfather gave it to her on their twentieth anniversary."

"It's beautiful," she said in a voice hardly above a whisper.

Jake took her left hand in his. "I botched my first proposal. I wanted to do this one right."

She curled her fingers into a fist, preventing him from slipping the ring on, and said gently, "I can't accept. The ring or your proposal. You know that."

He'd anticipated the possibility of her refusal and had come prepared to convince her to accept. "Why not? We're getting along really well."

"We are. But compatibility isn't enough of a reason to marry."

"It's a start. And giving my child my name is a hell of a good reason. So is supporting him. Taking care of him. Taking care of *you*."

Her shoulders sagged. "We have too many problems to work out before we can consider marriage."

"Not so many." His smile dissolved into a flat line.

"What about where to live?"

"My house is bigger."

"Mine is closer to the hospital if the baby needs constant attention."

"Fine. Your house. I'll commute to the ranch."

"What about the girls?"

"No problem. They like you."

"I meant, where would they sleep on the weekends? I don't have enough bedrooms."

"Sleeping bags on the living room floor."

"That'll go over big."

"Then we'll stay at my house on those weekends."

"What about the rest of your family?"

"Carolina thinks you're great."

"Your parents don't."

"That isn't true. My mom was really happy when we first started dating."

"Yeah, but back then I wasn't pregnant with a child that could have severe health issues. And you were in a slump because of Ellen's engagement. Your mother was glad to see you moving on. It didn't matter who with."

"She told me the other day how much she respects and admires you."

"Which isn't the same as being ecstatic at the prospect of us marrying."

Lilly tensed and moved away. Only an inch or two but Jake noticed.

"My parents will come around, just like the girls and Carolina have."

She shook her head. "How could we even have a wedding? I'm not allowed to stand up for longer than it takes to walk from the bedroom to the living room."

"We'll get married here. In the solarium."

"On the chaise longue?"

"Why not? We won't invite many people. Have a justice of the peace perform the ceremony."

"I don't want to get married lying down. And what about a dress?"

"Your mom will help."

"I want to pick out my own dress."

"We'll have a big wedding after the baby's born. Invite everyone from the center."

"That's a lovely idea, but no."

"Why wouldn't you invite them?"

She sighed as if he were being intentionally obtuse. "I meant no to a wedding, not to inviting the center's clients. Which, now that you mention it, is another concern of mine."

"The clients?"

"Kayla's uncomfortable around them, and the center is a large part of my life."

"She'll feel more comfortable in time."

"She's a little girl and can't control or evaluate her feelings."

"I'll get Jimmy Bob to help."

"He may have Down's syndrome but he's physically fit, capable of learning and able to function independently to a certain degree. Nothing like Evan. How do you think

Kayla will react to a brother with a misshapen head and shrunken limbs?"

"You're being unnecessarily harsh."

"I'm speaking from experience."

"I know she'll get over her fears."

"Brad could hardly bear to look at Evan. It tore me apart to watch them together. I can't go through that again."

"The fact is, none of this may come to pass."

"You can't know for sure until it happens." Lilly pushed up on one elbow. "And neither will I."

"I've supported you and stood behind you during this entire pregnancy. I've let you set the pace and call the shots, even when I didn't agree with you."

"And I appreciate that."

He suppressed his irritation. "This is my baby, too, Lilly. I have a right to make some of the decisions regarding him— or her. Including giving the baby my name."

She opened her mouth to speak, then promptly closed it.

"You can't do it all alone. You're going to need help," he said before she'd regained her composure. "*Especially* if the baby's born like Evan. I can be that help."

Her expression softened and for a moment, she was the Lilly he knew and understood. "I feel like I'm hurting you, and that's not my intent. But you're not facing reality. You have this fantasy of a perfect family. You and me, your daughters and our baby, all happy and healthy and loving."

"Don't you have the same fantasy?"

"Yes, on occasion. Then I remember what I went through with Evan and Brad."

"What exactly did your ex-husband do to you?"

"Besides disappoint me and abandon me when I needed him the most?"

"The death of a child should bring people closer together. It did for my parents, but I guess they're the exception."

"So was Brad, but not the way you think." Lilly's voice dropped to a hush. "Evan was only two months old—not nine—when Brad packed his bags and left me. He never visited the hospital again after he moved out. Although he called regularly, I didn't see much of him until Evan died. I was stupid enough to think he might want a reconciliation, but a week after the funeral, he served me with divorce papers."

Jake took a much-needed minute to recover. Lilly hadn't told him that part of the story. "I'm sorry, sweetie. It must have been awful for you."

"Awful doesn't come close to describing what I went through."

"I'm not like Brad. I won't leave you."

She turned tear-filled eyes to him. "Do you love me, Jake?"

"I...of course."

"I shouldn't have to ask you that or insist you tell me." Her smile was painfully sad.

"No, you shouldn't." He considered saying the words now but realized they'd sound shallow and forced and that wouldn't advance his cause. If only he'd said them at the hospital when he'd had the chance.

"We can be parents to this child without being in love," she said, folding her arms across her chest and hugging herself, "But we can't have a good marriage without it."

"I wouldn't have come here today with my grandmother's ring if I didn't love you."

"You asked me to marry you before—out of duty, not love."

"That was true once, but not anymore. I've changed since then." He wished he could convince her he meant what he said.

Her eyes pleaded with him to understand. "It would be different if we knew the baby was healthy."

"We *would* know if you'd consented to the tests when Dr. Paul first suggested them and it was safe."

She scowled and withdrew. "Now you sound like Brad."

Jake stood up, his boots hitting the tile floor with a thud. He could take pretty much anything she threw at him but he was tired of constantly being compared to her ex-husband.

"I don't get you sometimes." He shoved his grandmother's ring in his jeans pocket.

If Lilly saw him do that, she gave no indication. "How so?"

He swung around to face her. "You're doing exactly what you got mad at *me* for doing six months ago."

"Which is?"

"Slamming on the brakes just when the other person wants to step up the relationship."

"This is entirely different!"

"Why? Because you're the one doing the brake-slamming?"

"I have a good reason."

"You have lots of reasons. I'm beginning to wonder if you stay up at night thinking of them."

"That's not a very nice thing to say."

"I love you, Lilly. I want to marry you." Jake stepped toward the door, or, more accurately, was propelled to move by a surge of resentment. "You're right, I should've told you before, but I thought I was showing you how I felt by proposing."

"Jake, please don't leave like this." She pushed to a more erect position. "Can't we just keep going on the way were until after the baby's born? Then decide to get married?"

"There's something I've been wondering about you and Brad for a while now." He raked his fingers through his hair. "Did Brad really leave you?"

"Yes. Why would you ask me that?"

She looked so vulnerable, sitting on the chaise while he loomed over her. If he hadn't been so furious, if he hadn't risked his ego, only to be kicked to the curb, he might have kept his stupid mouth shut.

But Jake knew he didn't handle rejection well, in business or personally. He wouldn't keep asking Lilly to marry him, wouldn't keep offering to help her, only to be turned down. And he wouldn't leave her house today without saying what was really bothering him.

"I'm just wondering if maybe you misread the situation with Brad."

"I don't think it's possible to misread someone abandoning you." Her eyes flashed with indignation.

"Did he?" Jake started toward the door. "Or did he get tired of you always shutting him out?"

"Is that what you believe I did?"

"It's what you're doing to me, what you've been doing to me all along. And I'm finally getting the message."

She didn't try to stop him, not that he would've gone back. His pride wouldn't have let him.

He walked through the kitchen and was glad to encounter Claire, back from her errands. Angry as he was, he didn't like the idea of leaving Lilly alone.

Claire took one look at him and blurted, "Did something happen? Is Lilly okay?"

"She's fine."

"Are *you* okay?" she asked with concern.

He stopped in midstep. "Call me if you or Lilly need anything."

"That sounds like an I'm-not-coming-back line."

"Bye, Claire."

He nodded and left the woman he'd hoped would be his

mother-in-law. His thoughts, however, were on her daughter, the woman he'd hoped would be his wife.

How could something that had seemed so right a few hours ago turn so wrong?

Chapter Fourteen

"Physically, you're doing great." Dr. Paul packed her stethoscope into a black carrying case she'd set on the chest at the foot of Lilly's bed. "I'm thinking we can upgrade you to modified moderate bed rest. At least on a trial basis. See how it goes."

"What does that involve?" Anything sounded better than the strict bed rest Lilly had been on for three solid weeks.

"You can get up for four hours a day. Not one minute more." Dr. Paul wagged a warning finger at Lilly. "Two two-hour intervals. One in the morning, one in the afternoon. The remainder of the time, bed and couch. If you continue to do well, I'll consider increasing the four hours to six. But you have to be good."

"I will." Lilly felt like a newly paroled prisoner. "I promise."

"No exercise, no lifting, no carrying, no driving and no walking long distances. If you have to go someplace, someone takes you. Sit as much as possible."

The restrictions didn't leave Lilly many choices. Still, it was an improvement. Even sitting on a bench in the park up the road would be a refreshing change. Better yet, the one by the corrals at the ranch. She could watch the center's clients ride Big Ben.

On second thought, maybe that wasn't such a good idea.

What if Jake showed up? They hadn't spoken much since their argument last week. Though he called regularly to check on her, he talked mostly to her mother. The few times she'd answered the phone, the conversations had been short and stilted.

If only he hadn't proposed. They could have gone on the way they were until the baby was born.

And what way was that? Her holding him at arm's length?

What Jake accused her of was true. Lilly had spent a lot of time this last week thinking. Convalescence was good for that. And she'd concluded that she'd been fooling herself if she'd believed a man like him would be satisfied with the arrangement simply because it was what she wanted.

Not that it *was* the arrangement she'd wanted. She dreamed of the kind of close and loving marriage her parents had. And his parents. The kind of relationship she'd envisioned back when she and Jake had first started dating…

When she hadn't been afraid he'd leave her. Afraid he wouldn't love her as much as she loved him.

Fear ruled Lilly's life and had from the day she'd learned she was pregnant. Fear she'd miscarry. Fear the baby would be born like Evan. Fear Jake would abandon her like Brad. And as much as she wished she could conquer it, she couldn't. It ate away at her like acid, and she was powerless to stop it.

She told herself she'd refused Jake's proposal in order to protect him from hurt and give him an out. In truth, she was the one who wanted protection, who wanted an out. She who was afraid to make the commitment he did so easily.

But knowing the motivation behind her actions didn't change the outcome or bring her insight into how to fix it. But, oh, if only she *could* fix her relationship with Jake.

Because her greatest fear these days was that if the baby was born normal and healthy—as increasingly seemed to be the case—she would have pushed Jake out of her life, out of *their* lives, for nothing.

"Did you call Karen DeSalvo?" Dr. Paul asked.

"Who?" Lilly blinked to clear her head.

"She's the psychologist whose name I gave you at the hospital."

"No, I haven't."

Dr. Paul sent Lilly one of her trademark kind smiles. "I wish you would. She's very good and very compassionate."

"I'm fine."

"Is that why you drifted off for several minutes just now?" She patted Lilly's hand, the gesture doctorly. "What you're going through would depress anyone. For someone who's lost three children, it must be excruciating. The inactivity, the seclusion, the solitude, can't be helping." Dr. Paul scratched something on a piece of paper. "Talking to someone, learning what you can do to cope, might make the remaining weeks easier."

Lilly fingered the note with the name and phone number Dr. Paul gave her. "Now that I'm able to get up and out for a few hours a day, I'm sure my frame of mind will improve."

"I hope so. And that you'll continue to do well. Returning to strict bed rest can be rough once you've had a taste of freedom."

"I'll take it very easy so that doesn't happen."

"Forgive me for being nosy but, as my patient, your welfare, and that of your baby, is critical to me." Dr. Paul tilted her head inquiringly. "I'm curious to know if there's more to your despondency than the pregnancy."

"There isn't."

"Jake called me the other day."

Lilly pulse tripped. "He did?"

"He asked how you were doing."

"What did you tell him?"

"Nothing, of course. I'm prohibited by law, which I explained to him. His call, however, concerned me, especially when he indicated that you and he weren't talking much."

"We had an argument last week."

"Well, it's understandable and not unexpected. This is a trying period for both of you. Add to that the fact that your hormones are out of whack, you're on a variety of medications, several with significant side effects, and you've been confined to bed. No matter how sympathetic a man is, and Jake *is* sympathetic, he can't fully relate to what you're going through. He certainly can't if you don't discuss it with him."

She sighed. "I realize I need to quit dodging his phone calls."

"Karen DeSalvo can help you both. Please consider making an appointment."

"I will."

"I have to go." Dr. Paul patted Lilly's hand again before rising. "Remember, don't do too much on the outings. And if there's the slightest change or problem, call me immediately."

After a final exchange, Dr. Paul left. Lilly put the piece of paper with the psychologist's name and number on it aside. She would think about calling, but not today. First things first. She had two hours of freedom ahead of her and she knew exactly what she wanted to do with them.

"Mom!" she called, slowly sitting up. Her bare toes touched the carpeted floor.

"Honey, what are you doing?" Claire exclaimed on seeing her.

"I've been paroled. Sort of."

Lilly explained her modified bed-rest routine while she changed into regular clothes, combed and rebraided her hair and dabbed on a small amount of makeup. When she'd finished, her mood was better than it had been in weeks.

"I need you to drive me somewhere," she said.

"Where?" Claire answered.

Lilly's eyes sparkled back at her from the bathroom mirror. "I want to stop by work."

LILLY LIVED fifteen minutes from the center. She figured she could spend well over an hour there before having to return home and to the couch. Long enough to visit everyone and solve the one or two problems that surely needed her attention.

The streets and buildings she and her mother passed on the drive to Horizon looked a little strange to Lilly. Familiar, yet different somehow. It made her realize how much being confined to her house for weeks had affected her, and she appreciated her reprieve that much more.

It also made her miss Jake. He'd become a vital and intricate part of her life and, despite their argument, always would be. They'd created a child together, a healthy one, God willing, and would be forever tied to each other because of that, regardless of the outcome.

Had she been able to conquer her fears, overcome her mistrust, stop making excuses, their bond might not be one distanced by many miles and with communications conducted through third parties.

The thought was a sobering one.

And not her first in the week since Jake had left.

She'd blamed Brad for leaving her because it was easier than admitting her part in the demise of their marriage. Easier to hold her head high after the horrible manner in which he'd handled their divorce. She'd blamed him because, in her mind, he'd deserved it.

Jake wasn't anything like her ex-husband and Lilly couldn't believe she ever thought he was. He'd forced her to examine her former marriage and ask *what came first?* Brad's withdrawal or her pushing him away?

There were days Lilly wasn't sure which—and days she knew and didn't like the answer. Was it too late to change? She hoped not.

"We're here," Claire singsonged.

The sign in the parking lot triggered a sudden pang in Lilly's chest. It seemed as if she'd been away from the center for years instead of weeks. It wouldn't surprise her to find new faces among the familiar ones.

What she hadn't expected to see was a woman sitting behind her desk, head bent over a calculator. Shock rendered Lilly immobile. Her mother had to nudge her along.

"Lilly!" Miranda, guardian of the front entrance and first to notice everyone who came in, tumbled out of her chair. "You're back."

She was joined by nearly everyone in the room.

To Lilly's annoyance, they blocked Lilly's view of the woman seated at her desk. Standing on tiptoe didn't help.

"Careful," she warned Jimmy Bob in a gentle voice when he hugged her a little too exuberantly.

"Sorry. I missed you."

"I missed you, too. All of you." Her smile encompassed the entire room.

"Have you come back to work?" Apparently, Mr. Deitrich was having one of his good days because he recognized her.

"Not yet. I hope to after the baby's born." If she wasn't spending every day at the hospital. "I just came by for a short visit."

"Who the hell is *she?*" Miranda gave Claire a stern once-over.

Lilly might have asked the same question about the woman in her office.

Claire endured Miranda's scrutiny without flinching. "I'm Lilly's mother. I'm staying with her."

"Hi." Jimmy Bob greeted Claire as he did anyone who was a friend or the friend of a friend. He hugged her.

Claire hugged him back.

"Give the poor girl a break." Georgina pushed through the crowd. She'd waited while everyone else had their turn with Lilly. Now, she was demanding equal time. "Can I get you anything? Cold water or some coffee?" offered Georgina.

"A chair." Lilly rested a hand on her protruding stomach. "I'm supposed to sit as much as possible." The commotion generated by her return had tired her more than she'd expected.

"Come on." Georgina guided Lilly toward the back of the room.

"Mom, will you be okay?"

"Miranda's going to give me the grand tour." Claire slung an arm around her new buddy.

Lilly had to dole out three more hugs before she and Georgina escaped to a small seating area behind a partition. Clients sometimes used this corner when they were high-strung and needed a place to calm down.

Within seconds, the center and its occupants returned to normal.

Lilly sank into one of the straight-backed chairs. She would've liked to inquire about the center, how they were faring without her and *who* the woman in her office was. Georgina, however, insisted on finding out about Lilly.

"You doing okay?"

"Pretty good." Lilly summarized the last few weeks, focusing on her pregnancy and omitting anything about Jake. Georgina didn't appear to notice, but then Lilly had always been closemouthed with her co-workers when it came to him.

"I'm so glad. We've been worried sick about you. It must be incredibly difficult, being confined to bed."

"I'd say I'm getting used to it but I'd be lying."

"Please tell me you're coming back after the baby's born."

"I hope so."

Lilly wanted nothing more. There was a limit to the amount of medical leave she could take before she risked losing her job. The FMLA didn't apply in her case because the center employed less than fifty people. She was completely dependent on her boss's generosity. And though the baby came first, she needed an income. As it was, she'd been drawing on her retirement account to make ends meet, and that would only last so long.

Jake's pledge to take care of her and their child echoed in her head.

No. Supporting her wasn't an option. She'd made it on her own for years and wouldn't stop now. Helping with the baby's expenses, yes. That was different. And when he or she was born, Lilly would take Jake up on his promise.

There. She'd made a decision about the baby, and it wasn't as hard as she'd thought it would be.

"I can't believe how much this place has changed in such a short while," she told Georgina.

"It isn't the same without you."

Lilly couldn't hold her tongue any longer. "Who's the gal in my office?" She didn't add *my replacement*. Her heart ached just to think the words, much less speak them.

"Her?" Georgina's grin widened. "That's Alice. She's Jake's assistant from the ranch."

"Oh." Lilly hadn't recognized her. "What's she doing here?"

"I assumed you knew."

"Knew what?"

"She's been coming in every afternoon for the past week. To pick up the slack."

"You're kidding."

"No. She's pretty good, too. Not like you, of course, but who is?"

"Dave hired her?"

"Technically, she's a volunteer."

"That's very nice of her." Lilly was only casually acquainted with Jake's very efficient, very professional and not over-friendly personal assistant. "I wouldn't have pegged her as the type to volunteer."

"She's all right when you get to know her. Which is fortunate since she'll be here until you return. Jake arranged it."

"I'm confused."

"He pays her to work here."

"He does?"

"He comes in most afternoons, too."

"He does?" Realizing she sounded like a parrot, she shut up. Georgina fidgeted. "Did I mess up by telling you this?"

"No. Not at all." In all their conversations, which weren't many lately, Jake hadn't said anything about either of them helping out at the center.

"Good. Because he's been really great. And the girls, too."

"Girls?" Lilly wasn't sure she'd heard right.

"His daughters. The two youngest ones come in with him after school sometimes. Of course, they aren't much help, but they sure are cute and very entertaining. The clients love them."

"LeAnne *and* Kayla?"

"Yes."

Kayla! Who would have guessed?

"If you stick around a few minutes," Georgina said, "he'll probably show up."

"Really?" Lilly's hand went to her hair. How did it look? Had she chewed off her lipstick?

"That's not all he's done, either. Dave's been going crazy running both centers. He swore if you were out for another two weeks, he was going to replace you. Jake went to Dave and convinced him to keep your job indefinitely. In exchange, we get Alice. Jake's mother helps out, too, once a week. She does the filing and takes the deposit to the bank."

"His…mother?"

"Yeah. And whatever's left, he handles. I guess running Horizon isn't too different from running a guest ranch."

Lilly sat there, dumbstruck.

"He's a great guy, Lilly," Georgina said. "And absolutely nuts about you."

"You think so?"

"How many guys would pay their assistant *and* give up their afternoons to cover for you until you came back to work?"

"Not many."

"Damn straight."

Of everything Jake had ever done for her, this was the sweetest, the kindest, the most generous. He—and his daughters—had proved their willingness to make the center a part of their lives and do whatever it took to help Lilly.

Thank God he hadn't given up on her.

Her heart seemed to tighten, then expand as it filled to bursting with love for him and his family, every one of whom was dear to her. All the barriers she'd erected between her and Jake, all the excuses she'd made to maintain those barriers, fell away, leaving her exposed and vulnerable and finally able to give herself to him heart and soul.

"I'd better find Mom and bail her out." Bracing a hand on the table, Lilly stood. She felt suddenly light and unencumbered. It was true; she still had the same number of burdens to carry. But they weren't as heavy because she shared them with Jake. "Miranda's probably talked her ear off."

Claire was talking, all right. But with Jake, not Miranda. He'd apparently arrived while Lilly and Georgina were in the break room. He wasn't alone. A half dozen of the center's clients completed the circle surrounding him and Claire.

Lilly moved slowly into the room, observing him from a distance. He hadn't noticed her yet. No one had. They stared at him as if he'd hung the moon.

So did she.

In the next instant, he looked up and caught her watching him. Her breath lodged in her throat.

Something must have flashed in her eyes—or was it the involuntary step she'd taken?—because his smile went from expectant to ecstatic.

All at once, he was across the room, then standing beside her. Taking her in his arms, he held her as if she were everything in the world to him.

"I was wrong," she said, pressing her face into his neck.

"Me, too."

It was enough for now. Later, they'd sort out all the misunderstandings and take back the angry words they'd said.

"I love you, Lilly." He withdrew only enough to place his hand on her stomach. "You and the baby. And I always will, no matter what."

She didn't doubt him and never would again. "I love you, too."

"I'm hoping what they say is true." He reached into the front pocket of his jeans.

"What's that?"

"About the third time being the charm." He withdrew his grandmother's ring. "I've been carrying this everywhere with me. I didn't have the heart to put it away."

"Oh, Jake!"

"Will you marry me, Lilly? Be my wife and the mother of my child?"

Claire started crying. She wasn't the only one.

Tears sprang to Lilly's eyes, and her throat closed, which

made accepting Jake's proposal difficult. She finally managed a hoarse "Yes."

He slipped the ring on her finger. It fit as though it was made for her. The way she fit in Jake's life and he in hers. They sealed their commitment with a lingering kiss. She hardly heard the whoops and cheers from the center's clients and staff over the pounding of her heart, which was and would forever be joined with Jake's.

Epilogue

"Ladies and gentlemen, may I present Mr. and Mrs. Jake Tucker."

At the minister's announcement, the group of people on the porch of Founder's Cabin applauded. Lilly's lips still tingled from Jake's kiss, the one that had united them as husband and wife. On her finger, a simple gold band nestled beside his grandmother's sapphire ring.

They'd opted for a very small wedding, immediate family and a few friends, and had pulled it together in a matter of weeks. Still bedridden for most of the day, Lilly couldn't have managed without her mother, who'd stayed on, and Jake's mother, who was quite possibly the best mother-in-law in the world.

There was no reception line. Instead, everyone converged on the bride and groom, showering them with hugs, kisses and good wishes. Lilly knew she should lie down soon but was too excited.

"Come see Big Ben." Jimmy Bob, dressed in his groomsman's suit, beckoned Lilly and Jake to accompany him. "Me and Briana fixed him up."

He led the newlyweds to the porch railing. The old mule was tied to the hitching post in front of the cabin, a wreath of spring flowers on his neck. He was more interested in trying to eat them than showing them off.

"Thank you, Jimmy Bob." Lilly kissed his cheek. "And you, too." She embraced Briana and might have pulled back if the teenager hadn't continued to cling to her.

Of all the wedding presents Lilly had received, that was the best.

"Are you hungry?" Jake asked, stealing her away to a corner of the porch for a moment of privacy.

"Not really."

"Tired?"

"No, but I should be—"

An odd sensation, unlike any she'd previously felt during her pregnancy, rippled through her middle. Grimacing, Lilly held her stomach.

"Sweetheart, are you okay?"

"I don't think so." Suddenly, her water broke, soaking her dress and the porch floor. "Jake!"

Carolina rushed forward. "You two go. I'll take care of everything here."

He wasted no time helping her to his truck. Lilly knew as he buckled her in the front seat that there was no stopping this premature labor. She prayed that at thirty-three weeks, she was far enough along, and the baby would be safe.

Please, please.

The wedding guests gathered in front of the cabin and waved goodbye. Jake held Lilly's hand the entire way to the hospital and all through her labor, which lasted a mere forty minutes. If he hadn't driven like a madman, they might have become parents somewhere along the road to Payson.

"It's a girl," Dr. Paul said and lifted up a wriggling, squalling baby.

"A girl!" Lilly fought to sit up straight. "Is she all right?"

Jake was beaming. "She sure can cry."

Dr. Paul brought the baby over and laid her in Lilly's arms. "She's small but looks perfectly healthy. Do you hear me, Lilly? *Perfect.* Ten fingers and ten toes. You have your baby."

Lilly cradled her beautiful new daughter in one arm. The other, she wrapped around Jake.

"You're not sorry you have another girl?"

"Are you kidding?" He kissed the top of her head, then their daughter's damp brown hair. "Boys are overrated."

"What should we name her?" Lilly asked, laughing and crying at the same time. Finally, after all these years, she'd beaten the odds.

"I was thinking…."

"Yes?"

"Hailey, after my sister."

"And Claire, after my mother?"

"Hailey Claire Tucker," Jake said with pride, slipping his index finger into the baby's small fist. She instantly stopped flailing and looked at her parents with unfocused eyes. "I like the sound of that," he said.

"I like it, too."

Lilly gazed down at her daughter, then over at Jake. Joy bubbled up inside her. In one day, she'd become a wife *and* a mother.

"We did it," she said. "We have a baby."

"You did it."

All those pictures of ideal families she'd tried to imagine and couldn't suddenly came into sharp focus. Soon they'd be a reality. They'd cover the walls of the home she shared with the man she loved and the child she'd always wanted.

Lilly sighed contentedly. The wait had been worth it.

* * * * *

ALEXANDROS KAREDES, SNOW DUSTING the shoulders of his leather jacket and glittering like jewels in his dark hair, stood at the door. Maria felt the blood drain from her head.

"Good evening, Ms. Santos."

His voice was as she remembered it. Deep. Husky. Perfect English, but with the faintest hint of a Greek accent. And cold, as cold as it had been that awful morning she would never forget, when he'd accused her of horrible things, called her terrible names....

"Aren't you going to ask me in?"

She fought for composure. Last time they'd faced each other, they'd been on his turf. Now they were on hers. She was in command here, and that meant everything.

"There's a sign on the door downstairs," she said, her tone every bit as frigid as his. "It says, 'No soliciting or vagrants.'"

His lips drew back in a wolfish grin. "Very amusing."

"What do you want, Prince Alexandros?"

A tight smile eased across his mouth and it killed her that even now, knowing he was a vicious, arrogant man, she couldn't help but notice what a handsome mouth it was. Chiseled. Generous. Beautiful, like the rest of him, which made him living proof that beauty could, indeed, be only skin deep.

"Such formality, Maria. You were hardly so proper the last time we were together."

She knew his choice of words was deliberate. She felt her face heat; she couldn't help that but she damned well didn't have to let him lure her into a verbal sparring match.

"I'll ask you once more, your highness. What do you want?"

"Ask me in and I'll tell you."

"I have no intention of asking you in. Tell me why you're here or don't. It's your choice, just as it will be my choice to shut the door in your face."

He laughed. It infuriated her but she could hardly blame him. He was tall—six-two, six-three—and though he stood with one shoulder leaning against the door frame, hands tucked casually into the pockets of the jacket, his pose was deceptive. He was strong, with the leanly muscled body of a well-trained athlete.

She remembered his body with painful clarity. The feel of him under her hands. The power of him moving over her. The taste of him on her tongue.

Suddenly, he straightened, his laughter gone. "I have not come this distance to stand in your doorway," he said coldly, "and I am not going to leave until I am ready to do so. I suggest you stand aside and stop behaving like a petulant child."

A petulant child? Was that what he thought? This man who had spent hours making love to her and had then accused her of—of trading her body for profit?

Except it had not been love, it had been sex. And the sooner she got rid of him, the better.

She let go of the doorknob and stepped aside. "You have five minutes."

He strolled past her, bringing cold air and the scent of the night with him. She swung toward him, arms folded. He reached past her, pushed the door closed, then folded his arms, too. She wanted to open the door again but she'd be damned if she was going to get into a who's-in-charge-here argument with him. She was in charge, and he would surely see a tussle over the ground rules as a sign of weakness.

Instead, she looked past him at the big clock above her work table.

"Ten seconds gone," she said briskly. "You're wasting time, your highness."

"What I have to say will take longer than five minutes."

"Then you'll just have to learn to economize. More than five minutes, I'll call the police."

Instantly, his hand was wrapped around her wrist. He tugged her toward him, his dark-chocolate eyes almost black with anger.

"You do that and I'll tell every tabloid shark I can contact about how Maria Santos tried to buy a five-hundred-thousand-dollar commission by seducing a prince." He smiled thinly. "They'll lap it up."

* * * * *

What will it take for this billionaire prince to realize he's falling in love with his mistress...?
Look for
BILLIONAIRE PRINCE, PREGNANT MISTRESS
by Sandra Marton.
Available July 2009 from Harlequin Presents®.

We'll be spotlighting a different series every month throughout 2009 to celebrate our 60th anniversary.

Look for Harlequin® Presents in July!

TWO CROWNS, TWO ISLANDS, ONE LEGACY
A royal family, torn apart by pride and its lust for power, reunited by purity and passion

Step into the world of Karedes beginning this July with

BILLIONAIRE PRINCE, PREGNANT MISTRESS
by
Sandra Marton

Eight volumes to collect and treasure!

You're invited to join our Tell Harlequin Reader Panel!

By joining our new reader panel you will:

- Receive Harlequin® books—they are FREE and yours to keep with no obligation to purchase anything!
- Participate in fun online surveys
- Exchange opinions and ideas with women just like you
- Have a say in our new book ideas and help us publish the best in women's fiction

In addition, you will have a chance to win great prizes and receive special gifts!
See Web site for details. Some conditions apply.
Space is limited.

To join, visit us at

www.TellHarlequin.com.

REQUEST YOUR FREE BOOKS!

2 FREE NOVELS PLUS 2
FREE GIFTS!

Love, Home & Happiness!

YES! Please send me 2 FREE Harlequin® American Romance® novels and my 2 FREE gifts (gifts are worth about $10). After receiving them, if I don't wish to receive any more books, I can return the shipping statement marked "cancel." If I don't cancel, I will receive 4 brand-new novels every month and be billed just $4.24 per book in the U.S. or $4.99 per book in Canada.* That's a savings of close to 15% off the cover price! It's quite a bargain! Shipping and handling is just 50¢ per book. I understand that accepting the 2 free books and gifts places me under no obligation to buy anything. I can always return a shipment and cancel at any time. Even if I never buy another book from Harlequin, the two free books and gifts are mine to keep forever.

154 HDN EYSE 354 HDN EYSQ

Name _____ (PLEASE PRINT) _____

Address _____ Apt. # _____

City _____ State/Prov. _____ Zip/Postal Code _____

Signature (if under 18, a parent or guardian must sign)

Mail to the **Harlequin Reader Service**:
IN U.S.A.: P.O. Box 1867, Buffalo, NY 14240-1867
IN CANADA: P.O. Box 609, Fort Erie, Ontario L2A 5X3

Not valid to current subscribers of Harlequin® American Romance® books.

Want to try two free books from another line?
Call 1-800-873-8635 or visit www.morefreebooks.com.

* Terms and prices subject to change without notice. Prices do not include applicable taxes. N.Y. residents add applicable sales tax. Canadian residents will be charged applicable provincial taxes and GST. Offer not valid in Quebec. This offer is limited to one order per household. All orders subject to approval. Credit or debit balances in a customer's account(s) may be offset by any other outstanding balance owed by or to the customer. Please allow 4 to 6 weeks for delivery. Offer available while quantities last.

Your Privacy: Harlequin is committed to protecting your privacy. Our Privacy Policy is available online at www.eHarlequin.com or upon request from the Reader Service. From time to time we make our lists of customers available to reputable third parties who may have a product or service of interest to you. If you would prefer we not share your name and address, please check here. ☐

HAR09R

**Stay up-to-date
on all your romance
reading news!**

The Inside Romance
newsletter is a **FREE**
quarterly newsletter
highlighting
our upcoming
series releases
and promotions!

Go to
eHarlequin.com/InsideRomance
or e-mail us at
InsideRomance@Harlequin.com
to sign up to receive
your FREE newsletter today!

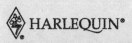
HARLEQUIN®

American ★ Romance®

COMING NEXT MONTH
Available July 14, 2009

#1265 BACHELOR CEO by Michele Dunaway
Men Made in America
When Chase McDaniel learns his position has been usurped by
Miranda Craig, the CEO apparent is stunned. He's devoted his whole life
to the family business—it's his legacy. But the more he gets to know his
gorgeous replacement, the more he wants the job *and* the woman who's
standing in his way. Is there room at the top for both of them?

#1266 A FATHER FOR JESSE by Ann Roth
Fatherhood
Emmy Logan came to Halo Island with her son to make a fresh start. But
what her boy really needs is a man in his life—someone who'll stick around.
Mac Struthers is *not* that man. After raising his two brothers, the last thing he's
looking for is another family. So why is the rugged contractor acting as if that's
exactly what he wants?

#1267 LAST RESORT: MARRIAGE by Pamela Stone
Charlotte Harrington needs to get married—quickly! With her grandfather
looking at every move she makes managing one of his hotels and a slimy
ex-boyfriend on the scene, Charlotte is desperate. And a fake marriage with
playboy Aaron Brody seems a harmless way to buy her some time—until she
falls in love with him.

#1268 THE DADDY AUDITION by Cindi Myers
Tanya Bledso has returned to Crested Butte to raise her daughter and run the
local community theater. She expected to find the same quiet, quirky small
town—but the place is bustling! And it's Jack Crenshaw who's responsible for
this mess. Tanya will tell her former high school sweetheart what she thinks of
his *development*…as soon as she conquers the attraction between them!

www.eHarlequin.com

HARCNMBPA0609